The Truth About Twelve

Theresa Martin Golding

Boyds Mills Press

Published by Boyds Mills Press, Inc.
A Highlights Company
815 Church Street
Honesdale, Pennsylvania 18431
Printed in China

Library of Congress Cataloging-in-Publication Data

Golding, Theresa Martin.
The truth about twelve / by Theresa Martin Golding.— 1st ed.
p. cm.
Summary: Tremendously burdened by a secret guilt, twelve-year-old Lindy uses her skill at baseball to help her cope with a new school, scornful classmates, and complicated family problems.
ISBN 1-59078-291-7 (alk. paper)
[1. Secrets—Fiction. 2. Emotional problems—Fiction. 3. Family problems—Fiction. 4. Guilt—Fiction. 5. Baseball—Fiction.] I. Title.

PZ7.G56775Tr 2004
[Fic]—dc22

2003026878

First edition, 2004
The text of this book is set in 13-point Minion.

Visit our Web site at www.boydsmillspress.com

10 9 8 7 6 5 4 3 2 1

In memory of my father, James J. Martin,
a man of great courage, compassion and intelligence,
who taught me the truth about many things

—T. M. G.

1

◆ ◆ ◆

IF I HAD ALWAYS LIVED HERE, I could blame what happened to my family on the gasoline fumes — diesel, unleaded, and super premium — that seep indoors from the cars and trucks that rumble past our drafty old house all hours of the day and night. But I didn't always live here. I came from another planet. At least, that's what it feels like most days. And keeping my secret is getting harder all the time.

I stuck my head out the bedroom window and tasted the morning exhaust. It was light, with a touch of dampness, not too cold. I swear, if my arm were about six inches longer, I could touch one of those tractor-trailers. With a good jump, I could land on the top and get a ride out of Shelbourne all the way back to Philadelphia, where I belong.

I sat on the windowsill and leaned my whole body out, flirting with the idea. If I could only get my family back to Philadelphia, I just know that everything would be like it used to be. Even though it's been almost a year since we've been gone, I decided to write to Andy Carlucci again to ask him if our old house was still empty. And this time, I'm really going to mail the letter. What do I care if he asks me questions about what happened that day? I don't have to tell him anything. I bet he would ask me flat out if it was all my fault. It's a question that worries me. It's a question that no one has asked me yet. I could always lie.

The truth of what I did that day used to burn inside me like a fire. But over the past year, it has settled down into the pit of my stomach like a big bowling ball, cold and hard. I just can't bring it up. Some days it presses down on me so, I can hardly get out of bed.

A pair of dusty, gray trucks whipped past my window, flinging gravel and coughing black smoke. I watched the dirty cloud drift over our house and slowly sink into the yard. There was a loud clank of metal from below and then a sharp cry.

"Dad?!" I yelled. "Are you down there?" I froze for a second, listening, foolishly hoping that he might actually answer me. I ducked back inside and flew down the steps. I burst onto the porch and jumped into the yard in my bare feet.

"What happened?" I panted.

He looked up, like he was just slowly waking from

some dream, trying to figure out where he was. "Nothing happened."

"But I thought I heard a . . . Look at your hand!" I cried. "You're bleeding!" I ran back inside and grabbed a wet towel and one of those oversized Band-Aids.

When I came out, he was back at work on his new project like nothing had happened, junk scattered all around him in the grass. His blood was dripping, mixing with the grease on some old pipe that he must have found out on the highway. I took his hand and dabbed at the wound with the clean towel. He didn't even flinch.

Dad's hands are real big and rough. He's got calluses and scars all over, and one of his fingers is even missing half a nail from an accident at work years ago. Andy Carlucci said once that it looked like my dad had monster hands. I pushed him so hard he fell backwards onto the sidewalk. I loved the way my Dad's hands felt, especially when I was little and we went on long walks together. With my hand in his, I knew I was safe from every bad thing in the whole world, and I wouldn't have been scared even if we had run into a nine-hundred-pound lion in the middle of Fairmount Park.

"Don't worry, I'm almost done." I unwrapped the Band-Aid and carefully smoothed it over his cut. He gave my hand a quick squeeze and went right back to work. I wish every wound was that easy to fix.

I sat in the grass and leaned against him, looking around our crazy yard. When we lived in Philadelphia, Dad worked in a machine shop, and he's real good at making things. But lately, I kind of wonder where he's getting his ideas from. The tree in our yard has a full coat of armor on its trunk made entirely out of hubcaps, just in case a tree war breaks out in the neighborhood, I guess. There's a tin can-twisted metal sculpture over by the bushes that I still haven't figured out. Worst of all, back by the fence, there's an old flagpole that's got little square shelves, like steps, running up either side, and the head of a lady mannequin stuck up on top staring out at the traffic. Sometimes he puts birdseed on those shelves. Sometimes he fills them with old sneakers. Last week there was a perfect round orange on each shelf. I stole one for my lunch.

Dad used to talk a lot and tell me all about everything he was doing. He even let me use his tools, and once I fixed the washing machine all by myself. But now, I'm not even sure he knew I was here. And for about the one-millionth time I thought of telling him the truth about that day. Maybe if I told him, if he knew that it was all my fault and not his, he would come back to us, and be the same as before. But I am a coward. A lump rose in my throat.

I pretended that I needed to adjust the Band-Aid. I slipped my hand into Dad's and felt the familiar rough creases and callused edges of his palm. But it's not the same. I don't feel safe anymore. Now he's the one who needs protecting, and I just keep letting him down.

"Lindy!" Randy hissed through the screen door in his little voice. "The phone is for you!"

"Me?!" I jumped up. "Are you sure?"

He nodded his head, blond curls bouncing up and down emphatically.

I trudged inside and walked slowly toward the receiver. "Who is it?"

Randy shrugged.

We have lived here for five months and, though it has taken a lot of hard work, I have managed to keep the location and condition of our home a complete secret. I always give the wrong address and phone number to anyone who asks. If any of my classmates ever saw how I lived, I would have to wear a bag over my head for the rest of my life. Mostly, though, I keep the secret for Dad's sake. They just wouldn't understand him. Besides, I already accidentally mentioned to my friends that my dad was a big corporate executive. It was right after Eric said that his dad was in Japan on business and Melissa bragged that her dad was in New York working on some important court case. Then there was that little moment of silence when they looked over at me. I couldn't tell them that my dad was out on the bypass somewhere scouring the shoulder for discarded auto parts.

I sighed and stared at the phone in my hand. Maybe I should just hang up, pretending it was a wrong number. "Did you say I was home?" I whispered to Randy.

He bobbed his head again and grabbed hold of my one free hand. I shook him off. "Hello?" I finally said.

"Hi, Lindy!" Kelly O'Brien's cheerful voice boomed into my ear.

"Kelly! How did you get my phone number?" Kelly is just about the nicest person I know in Shelbourne, but I can't trust anybody here.

"Caller ID," she chirped. "You called me for those math answers on Thursday night, remember? Guess what? My mom said that we can pick you up and take you to practice today. Want to? She can give you a ride home, too, and we can stop for ice cream."

My mouth froze in the open position for a minute. Randy was staring up at me and standing so close he was like my third leg. I shoved him away again. "I, um, you can't," I finally mumbled. "It's because the . . . the street is being fixed. It's all torn up. No cars can get down."

"No way! What happened?" Kelly asked.

"I don't know. Some big gas leak or something. It's real dangerous. There are like cop cars and fire engines all over the place. You'd better not come near here. I can just walk anyway. It's not far."

"Oh. OK. Maybe you can come for ice cream afterward."

"Yeah, maybe. Thanks. See you later." I hung up. Maybe in a million years.

Randy stood beside the couch, a safe two or three feet away from me, his eyes wide and panic-stricken. "What's dangerous, Lindy?"

"Nothing! Nothing is dangerous."

"But you said . . . "

"I was just making up a story, OK? So knock it off. Go watch TV."

He picked at the side of the couch. "But I don't want

to," he sniffed, looking down at his old sneakers, the laces untied. That boy still didn't know how to tie a shoe.

"Just do it."

"But, Lindy . . . "

I didn't have time for his moping. I had too much thinking to do. I checked on Dad, still bent over his project, then stomped past Randy up to my room. I pulled my T-shirt up over my nose to filter out some of the fumes and leaned out the window again. It's really not all that far to Philadelphia. Why does it feel like a million miles away? I started to compose my letter to Andy in my head. "Dear Andy, So, how's it going? Sorry I didn't write sooner, but I've been soooo busy. Things are awesome here. Shelbourne is amazing. Everybody here is rich. We live in a big, fancy house, and the kids at my school are so cool. How's the old neighborhood? Have you been past my old house much? Did you notice if anyone . . . "

Somebody poked me in the back and I almost took that truck ride before I was planning to.

"Randy!" I screamed, whirling around on him. "Will you stop sneaking up on me all the time! You almost made me fall out the window!"

Randy did that little body droop he always does when I yell at him, like a dog that just got kicked. I hate that. It makes me so mad I feel like really kicking him. Sometimes I do. But today I settled for scolding him instead. "Didn't you ever hear of knocking?"

Randy started to sniffle. I swear, that boy's got the leakiest eyes that God ever made. All you have to do is look at him the wrong way and the waterworks start. Mom is always reminding me of how little he is. He's too young to understand everything that happened, she says, but old enough to feel the hurt. Be patient with him.

It's weird when you're twelve. Adults think you're a big kid, and you're supposed to understand everything they do and say. But the truth about twelve is that it's the year when you first start to figure out that nothing makes any sense. Adults, who you thought knew everything, can be really stupid sometimes. Presidents can be bad and get in trouble. The TV weatherman is about as accurate as that groundhog in Punxsutawney. And awful things can happen on an ordinary day and change your life forever.

Randy's sniffles had turned into a full-scale waterfall, and I figured I'd better do something quick before a lake started to form right there on my bedroom floor.

"Hey, Randy, do you want to make my bed for me?" I asked, like I was offering him some grand prize.

He wiped his nose on his sleeve and managed a small smile. "OK."

Poor kid. He thought that helping me with my chores was a great privilege. You couldn't help feeling sorry for him.

While Randy struggled with the sheets, I hunted for my softball glove. I'm not exactly the neatest person in the world. When Mom comes in my room she says it looks like the closet got sick and threw up all over my floor. I tell her not to get too upset with the closet. Being stuck living in this house makes me nauseous, too. Would you rather be back in "That Place"? That's Mom's answer to every one of my complaints. It makes me shut up right away because I would rather jump off a bridge than ever go back to "That Place." She knows it, too. The four months I lived there were the worst four months of my life.

This is another piece of age-twelve knowledge. Short of your being dead, grown-ups think you should be happy about all the rotten things that happen to you. If you have to wear your brother's old jacket to school, you should just be happy that you even have a coat. If your backpack has a picture of Barney the singing purple dinosaur on it, you should just be happy you don't have to carry your books to school in a grocery bag. If a cold wind whistles through your bedroom at night and the traffic noises won't let you sleep, you should just be happy that you have a roof over your head. I tried using that same logic on my mother last week when I came home with a D on my science test. I told her that she should just be happy that I didn't fail. But she didn't get happy at all. I hope now she knows how I feel. But I doubt it.

I was searching through a pile of clothes in the corner when Randy found the glove. It was stuffed under the covers at the foot of my bed.

"You got practice, Lindy?" he asked.

"Yeah. In about half an hour."

"Can I come? I'll be done making your bed."

"Aww, Randy. It's just a practice. Can't you stay home for once?" When you're a new kid trying to fit in at the middle school, it doesn't help your popularity any to have your six-year-old brother following you around everywhere you go — especially if he's the weepy kind who still sucks his thumb in public.

Randy looked away from me and his lower lip started to tremble. Sometimes I wish he'd throw fits and scream and shout. It would be a whole lot easier to walk out on him. But all his crying is totally silent.

I sat on my bed and pulled him onto my lap. He's puny for his age, with little stick legs and arms. You can just see all the scaredness right there in his big, watery blue eyes. Even though it's been almost a whole year, he's afraid they're going to take him away again. I must have told him one thousand times that it's not going to happen, but he's still afraid to be alone. Mom's not much help because she has to work a lot of double shifts. When she isn't working, she's trying to get a few hours of sleep. Freddy's just plain useless. He's practically never home anyway. Mom says he's just being a typical teenager. If that's what's going to happen to me — become Freddy-like — then I think I'll just skip my teenage years and go right to my twenties.

And then there's Dad. But he's not exactly a comfort to anyone. So that leaves me. I wrapped my arms around Randy and held him tight for a minute. "Are you sure you don't want to stay home this one time?" I asked.

I felt his head nodding against my chest. "OK, then," I sighed, setting him back on the floor. "Go get your jacket."

At least it was Saturday morning. We should be able to escape our property unseen by anyone from Mecong Middle School. A simple Plan A exit should work quite nicely.

"SHE CALLED AGAIN," Randy said.

He was waiting for me on the living-room couch, his shoes dangling from his feet, his body disappearing in the cushions. I swear that couch is the scariest piece of furniture that ever was. I never sit on it. It was a donation and I'm supposed to just be happy that we have a couch. But I'm not. It's big and old and the cushions have an evil sucking action that pulls you in so far that you can't even stand up on your own. I bet there are bones of innocent people deep down in there, people who sat down one day and got stuck, slowly starving to death, with nobody around to pull them out.

"Who called?" I tied Randy's shoes in double knots and yanked him to his feet.

"That girl. She says, 'Where is the gas weak?' She asked me what street we live on. She says she can pick you up."

"What?!" A hot flash of panic raced through me and I shoved Randy back onto the couch. "Why didn't you call me?" I yelled at him.

"You were in the bathroom," he whimpered, his arms and legs flailing in the air. "Get me up!"

"What did you tell her?"

"I don't know what a gas weak is. What is a gas weak?"

"Did you give her our address?" I demanded, my voice rising with each word.

Randy paused, then answered in a whisper. "I told her we live at Fif Street."

I grabbed his arm and pulled him to his feet. Good old Randy. He still has the Philadelphia street address stuck in his little mind. "FifTH Street," I corrected with a small smile. "But don't ever talk to my friends again when I'm not there. You got it?"

He bit his lower lip and nodded. Randy and I headed out to the backyard-front yard. I still haven't decided what to call it. This old house used to be part of a farm, but there's no telling anymore which side of it was supposed to be the front. I'm guessing that the front door is the one we can't open because it would smack right into the stockade fence that separates our house from the highway. I figure that highway was probably just a dirt road about a hundred years ago with carriages and horses clopping around, and the people who lived here just opened up their front door and waved hello to their neighbors. If I tried doing that today, I'd lose my hand and maybe even my whole arm.

The other door in our house leads from the kitchen out onto a crooked old porch with a view of the backyard-front yard. The yard's shaped like a piece of pie with wild and overgrown bushes all along its border and a gravel driveway snaking out at the very tip. I'm guessing that the fields were out that way and, with the bushes trimmed low, the farmer could stand on the porch and watch his crops grow or yell at his kids for throwing dirt at each other. The only things sprouting out there now in those old fields are a bunch of gigantic houses. I swear, each house is so big that a whole family of dinosaurs could live inside and not even bump into each other once.

Randy started to suck his thumb as soon as he saw Dad. "Just cut that out," I warned, "or I won't let you come with me. Go in and get Dad's jacket."

Randy ran inside, the screen door slamming behind him. I stood there and watched Dad work. He was still strong in some ways. He and I could probably even walk back to Philadelphia together. I figure it wouldn't take more than a couple of days. We could camp beside the highway. I could take him back to the rec center and the park. We could buy Cokes at the corner store and walk our favorite streets. Everybody would be happy to see my dad again. It would be just like the old days. In no time at all, he would be back to himself. I wish now that I had never asked Freddy to give us a ride in his old, dirty car. I should have known the rotten sneak would tell Mom about my plans. We should have just walked.

Randy came back out with the jacket, holding it up to me with his right hand, his left thumb buried deep in his mouth. I didn't even yell at him. Randy doesn't understand what happened to Dad and I don't think Mom or Freddy really do, either. But I understand, and it's not just because of age-twelve knowledge. It's because I was there when it happened. Just Dad and me. And when it was over, when we knew that there was nothing we could do to make it better, it was like Dad just stepped off the edge of some cliff. I've been trying to figure how to get him back up ever since.

I slipped Dad's arms into his jacket and zippered him up. Even though it was spring, it was too cold to be out in just a T-shirt.

"Randy and I are going to practice," I said. "How's that cut?"

He looked down at his hand, flexing his fingers.

"It's OK."

"You're sure it didn't need stitches or anything?"

He gave me a little smile. It was a joke and he got it. Dad was never one for going to the doctor or taking any medicines. He just trusted in Mother Nature and weathered everything on his own. The jagged skin would eventually heal and become the latest addition to his patchwork of scars. His hands were like a work of art. That's the way I always thought of them.

I've learned this past year, though, that wounds on the inside don't heal up in the same way. I've heard Mom's voice at night, crying sometimes, begging Dad to go to the doctor and maybe get some pills to help him through. I never hear his answers, but I know he's never gone. I don't know whether he's still waiting around for Mother Nature or whether he just knows that no pill will ever be able to change what happened.

"Randy," I called. "Go in again and get me the brush."

Dad's hair was a mass of tangles. He used to be so proud of that hair. Mom says it was plain old vanity. It took me till I was twelve to figure out that she meant that he was a little too much in love with his own reflection in the mirror. But I swear anybody who had hair like that would be vain. I was the only kid I knew who had a dad with long hair, and I thought it was so cool. How many other little girls got to play hair salon with their dads? Every night before I went to bed, he would brush out my hair and then let me brush his while he told a story. Even now that I'm twelve, whenever I hear a fairy tale my scalp starts to tingle.

Dad's hair is a perfect golden blond color and I swooped it back from his forehead and tucked it behind his ears. It curled up naturally just at his shoulders. There's some gray in it now, but it is still the most beautiful hair I have ever seen.

Dad had some kind of rusty gear in his hands and he was working at getting the handle off. He slowed down a bit while I brushed. You could always tell a whole lot about how Dad was feeling by watching his hands and the way they worked at things. It's been almost a year since the Awful Thing, and Dad's hands are getting more frantic by the day. I can see it building up in him like a volcano getting ready to blow.

I put my hand on his shoulder. "We'll be back in a little bit, then," I said. "OK?"

His hands were black. They gripped and twisted the old gear, wrestling it against the ground. He didn't answer, but I knew it was because he was somewhere else.

Randy and I headed down the driveway. I had to hold on to the back of his shirt because you never knew when he was going to forget himself and just plain walk out into the neighborhood. Since Randy is only six and has no friends, he doesn't understand the extreme importance of keeping the location and condition of our home a complete secret. True, it is one thousand times better than That Place we used to be in. But that is no comfort. I shudder every time I think about what would happen if Melissa Weatherfield and her group of friends found out where I lived. I might as well just go out and hang myself.

"Agent 006," I whispered to Randy, pulling him back beside the bushes. "Your mission is to check both sides of the street for enemies and report back to base. Any questions?"

Randy got into this game. His shook his head and dropped to his knees, crawling to the edge of the bush and looking up and down the street. He gave me the all-clear sign, but I double-checked the situation myself. Agent 006 means well, but I don't think he's cut out for a life of spying. I saw the McDavids' van backing out of their driveway, and I waited until it got to the stop sign and made a right on Windy Hollow Road. The McDavids only have two preschoolers, but you never know who they might be related to. I can't be too careful.

"Ready?" I squeezed Randy's hand. "Go!" We sprinted between the bushes, off the gravel path, and onto the gleaming, smooth sidewalk of the River Meadows development. It was warming up to be a beautiful spring day, and we strolled past all the picture-perfect houses just as though we belonged here. If you looked back, you couldn't even tell that our house was there. All you could see was a small gravel path disappearing into some tall, overgrown bushes.

I never thought I'd fall in love with shrubbery. But I swear I have.

RANDY AND I WANDERED through the twisty streets toward old man Weischak's cul-de-sac. We'd have called it a dead-end street in the city, but in the suburbs they have a different name for everything.

I kept a sharp eye out for Kelly's light blue van. If she talked her mom into cruising the local neighborhoods looking for me, I'd have to be ready to dive behind some bushes. I scouted the street ahead of me, noting the best places to hide. I also started collecting stones and pebbles and sticking them in my pockets.

"You're not goin' to throw stuff at the dogs again, are you?" Randy's little eyebrows scrunched together real tight.

"It's just in case," I told him. "For self-defense."

"But Mrs. Petra says the dogs are stuck behind the

Invisible Fence and they can't get us." Randy tried to pry the stones out of my hand. "She's gonna call the police and get you put in the jail if you do it again!"

I sighed. Randy wouldn't understand even if I explained it ten thousand times. I don't believe in anything invisible, not ghosts or spirits or curly-haired little guardian angels. And certainly not in fences made of air that are supposed to stop two hungry dogs from biting your legs off for their lunch. I decided to impart just a little of my twelve-year-old knowledge to Randy, but I knew it wouldn't work. It was like pouring water in a sieve. His head just wasn't ready to hold this kind of information. He kept jumping at me to get the stones. I slapped his hands away and held him by the shoulders.

"Randy," I explained in my best lecturing voice, "Mrs. Petra is a grown-up. Grown-ups do not always tell the truth." Randy started to squirm. "I know it's hard to believe. I probably wouldn't have believed it either when I was six. Some grown-ups tell even more lies than kids."

Randy's bottom lip started to quiver.

"I promise you Mrs. Petra is not going to call the police. She is just saying those things to scare me." I let go of him and started walking fast.

Randy jogged after me. "But what if she does?" That boy is hopeless. His eyebrows were still all knotted up and I could tell he was ready to bust into tears at any moment.

We rounded the corner and there it was — old man Weischak's cul-de-sac. It was like a picture in a magazine. It made Cinderella's castle look downright plain. No one would ever guess the dangers that lurked here. Three perfect houses big enough for dinosaur families all faced a circular street. There was not a weed in sight. Everything smelled of flowers and fresh mulch and chemical sprays. The grass was so green and thick that I rolled in it a few weeks back just to make sure it was real. That's when old man Weischak came after me with his stick. I don't even know why he needs a house when he spends all his time outside in the landscaping. He was probably lurking behind some bush right now, just waiting for an unsuspecting trespasser.

Right between Mr. Weischak's giant house and Mrs. Petra's giant house is a little gravel path that leads through some woods and out onto the ball fields behind Mecong Middle School. As soon as I step one foot on that path, Mrs. Petra's rabid, hairy black dogs start licking their chops. If I back away onto Mr. Weischak's lawn, he comes after me with his stick. But since I don't have a car and I live too close for the bus, this is the only way to get to the school. Someday I know that I will be found bleeding to death on this path, missing an arm or a leg and with several stick marks imprinted on my face. If I actually owned anything, I would make out my Last Will and Testament.

Randy was sniffling. I couldn't help it; I gave him a quick slap between the shoulder blades to toughen him up. Those two man-eating dogs suddenly got to their feet. Their lips curled back and the sun glinted off their razor-sharp teeth. "Don't move," I ordered in a quiet voice to

Randy. I slowly bent down to grab two handfuls of gravel from the path. I was breathing fast. Out of the corner of my eye I checked out the situation to my left, and it couldn't have been worse. Mr. Weischak appeared in the side yard with a giant pair of dangerous-looking shears. He pretended to be clipping his bushes, but I knew that he was really just watching me. Maybe I should have accepted that ride from Kelly. I pondered which would be worse: death by humiliation or death by dog bites. It was too close to call.

"Randy," I whispered, "stay close to me." But I could see he was losing it. He was dancing around like he had to go to the bathroom real bad.

"Stop that!" I hissed. "You're getting those dogs all excited." I could see the drool dripping from their jaws.

Every few seconds there was an ominous snip from Weischak's yard.

"We'll have to make a run for it," I told Randy. "When I say . . ."

Randy took off down the path, his arms flailing.

"Wait!" I called. "Not yet!" But it was too late.

Randy was running right into the thick of it, screaming, "Invisible Fence! Invisible Fence! Invisible Fence!" as though it was some kind of magic chant that would save his life.

The dogs went wild and streaked toward the path. I heard Weischak yelling and saw the glint of those shears getting near to Randy. I let out a blood-curdling yell like an Indian warrior and took off after my brother, hurling gravel right and left. The dogs backed off Randy and made right for me, snapping at my legs, growling and barking. Weischak was behind me somewhere, hollering. I ran out of gravel and started emptying my pockets of every stone I had, throwing blindly while I ran. I thought I was done for. I half didn't even know which way I was going. My heart was beating so fast that even my eyes were throbbing. But then I saw the woods coming up fast and I sprinted full speed. Randy was standing there in the shade wringing his hands, his face whiter than a birch tree. I collapsed on the ground next to him and tried to catch my breath.

"See, Randy?" I panted. "What did I tell you? Mrs. Petra didn't call the police."

"Mrs. Petra wasn't home" was all he said, dropping to the ground beside me.

I rested my head on my knees. There was dog drool on my legs and Weischak may have snipped off some of my hair, but other than that I made it in one piece. When I do get eaten by those dogs, I don't want Randy to see it. He's already got too much stuff to deal with and he'd end up over the cliff with Dad. He's not tough like me.

I heard shouts and laughter coming from the fields, and I figured I was late for practice again. I was in for another lecture in punctuality from my coach, Mrs. Tremont. I'll bet she's never had to walk the Path of Death just to get to practice.

"Let's go." I pulled Randy to his feet and we trudged through the last bit of woods and out onto the back edge of the school grounds. A big wooden sign next to the scoreboard read Welcome to Patriot Fields. Every time I see that sign I get a picture in my head of a bunch of minutemen running around the bases with muskets strapped to their backs. It's a stupid name for a ball field, but it gave me an idea for a quick Randy lesson.

"Hey, Randy," I said, "do you know why they call this place Patriot Fields?"

"Uh-uh." Randy shook his head. He didn't look much interested. His eyes were trailing in the grass, looking for bugs. He has a pet bug collection, but they're always dying or eating each other, so he needs new bugs every day.

"It's because George Washington played baseball here."

Randy looked up. "He did?"

"Yep. He was a first baseman, just like me."

I could see the wheels turning in Randy's head. George Washington did spend a lot of time around here, and Randy knows that. We've been to the Washington Crossing State Park just down the road, and kids who live in old historic houses are always saying that they found wooden teeth in their cellars.

Randy plucked a ladybug from my shirt and cupped it in his hand. "How could he play baseball when he was fightin' in a war?"

"He played on his days off," I explained. "There was no fightin' on Saturdays or Sundays. That's when they had the big baseball tournaments."

"Oh." Randy watched the ladybug crawl up his arm. Sometimes he's so stupid, it's annoying.

"Guess who played second base?"

"I don't know."

"His horse."

Randy smiled. It gave me some hope he might be catching on. He's just got to learn about lying. He's way too trusting.

"Horses can't play baseball," he giggled.

"This one could. He caught line drives in his mouth and he stopped grounders with his hooves."

Randy paused and looked up at me.

"Could he bat, too?"

I felt like hitting him again. I am doing my best to toughen that boy up by lying and tricking him whenever I can. He just never seems to learn.

I gave it one more try. "He swung the bat with his tail and then he galloped around the bases. He scored more runs than anybody else on the field."

"Wow!" Randy exclaimed. "I wish I could have a horse like that."

I couldn't help myself; I had to slap him. "Don't be so stupid," I scolded. "Horses can't play baseball." Even with all my training, Randy believes everything he hears, and he can't tell a simple lie to save his life. He still wishes on stars and crosses his fingers for good luck. He is like a baby with his eyes closed to the world. I don't want him to have to grow up all in one day, like I did. It hurts way too much. One minute, you're just a regular kid and everything is normal. The next minute, a ton of bricks gets dropped on your chest and you see what the world is really like. I'm trying to throw Randy just one brick at a time to make it easier, but he doesn't get it.

Randy did his little body slump and dragged his feet along the ground. I know he thinks I'm being mean. But I'm not. I'm doing him a big favor. I wish somebody had done this for me when I was six.

"Lindy!" Kelly was waving her arms at me. "Hurry up!"

I grabbed Randy by the shirt and we ran the rest of the way. I deposited him on the dirt pile behind the backstop and took my place on first base.

Mrs. Tremont was on the pitcher's mound. She crossed her arms and gave me that squinty-eye look. One day I think I'll suggest that she just tape record her punctuality lecture instead of wasting her time yelling at me every practice. "Lindy, you are late for practice again. What exactly is your problem?"

"The Path of Death, Mrs. Tremont. It's not my fault."

"The path of what?"

I knew she wouldn't understand. "The Path of Death. I almost got eaten by two vicious dogs back there. They're as big as lions and I barely got away. I've got dog drool on my legs. I had to fight them off with stones and . . . "

Mrs. Tremont held up her hand. "Lindy, I've heard of dogs eating children's homework, but never of dogs eating softball players."

"It's true!" I insisted. "You can even ask Randy."

Everyone turned and looked at my brother. He was not going to be a very convincing witness. He was digging for bugs in the big dirt pile the ground crew keeps around for spreading on the infield. Except for his curly blond head, he was covered with the fine powdery dirt and was as brown as the bugs he was looking for. There was a low rumble of laughter.

Mrs. Tremont turned back to me. "That won't be necessary. But if you want to play on this team, Lindy, you had better start coming to practice on time. Now let's play."

Mrs. Tremont often threatens to kick me off the team. But she never will. I am the best player she has. I'll never forget the look on her face that first day of tryouts back in late February. I'd only been at the school a little over two months. Even though Kelly was nice to me from the first day and included me in everything she did with her friends, I was still the new kid. Nobody paid much attention to me. I stood off to the side by myself, a tryout number pinned to my back. I think it was 16, but I felt like a zero. The fields were muddy and dotted with the remains of a melting snow, so we batted in the empty parking lot behind the school. I waited my turn, my hands shoved in my pockets to keep them warm. I knew the building was too close for me, but I just watched quietly as kid after kid stood at the plate and took their swings, each hit thudding safely onto the blacktop.

By the time my turn came, most kids weren't even watching anymore. They were talking in small groups or jumping around trying to keep warm. Maybe Mrs. Tremont lobbed it in to me because I was new and she wanted to give me a chance. I don't know. But when that ball floated over the plate, I cracked it hard. It was still traveling pretty fast when it crashed through the second-floor window of the science lab. Everybody got real quiet, but their mouths were hanging wide open. They all looked from me to the window and back again. And then suddenly I was a hero. If I had only known that breaking a window would get me accepted like this, I would have done it on my first day at Mecong. Mrs. Tremont stood frozen on the blacktop staring at me like she had just found a big diamond in the bottom of her cereal box.

This game is so easy that I cannot understand why everyone can't do it. It just baffles me why some people can't hit a ball that is as big as a grapefruit. I have suggested to Mrs. Tremont that we play stickball a few times so that everyone will realize how big and simple to hit that softball is. But she never pays any attention to my suggestions.

Kelly was at the plate, and she definitely would benefit from my ideas. She always looks as though she's afraid that the ball is going to hit her and knock her brains out. She bats in the ninth position and gets called out on strikes way too often. Mrs. Tremont was lobbing them in to her.

Kelly finally hit a weak grounder toward third and took off for first. Mae Janson scooped it up and rifled it to me. Mae has an arm like a rocket and she never misses. The ball smacked into my glove at about fifty miles per hour, and Kelly wasn't even halfway to the bag. She kept running hard, though, so I opened my glove and let the ball drop out. It rolled a bit toward second and I made a lame attempt to retrieve it, fumbling around just long enough for Kelly to be safe.

Mrs. Tremont glared at me, her left eyebrow arched high.

"Sorry," I called. But I wasn't and she knew it.

"Nice hit," I said to Kelly.

"Thanks," she puffed.

Brigid was up. She hits them hard, but always in the same place.

"If it's in the air, don't run," I warned Kelly, "or I'll catch you off the bag."

She crouched down in a running position, her hand on her knee. "So where were you last night?"

Kelly has bright orange hair, which she always wears pulled back in a short ponytail, and so many freckles that they seem to cover almost every inch of her skinny little face. She's the best friend I have in Shelbourne, which means I have to lie to her about ten times more often than I do to anyone else.

"Oh, yeah. Last night," I drawled. "My grandmother got sick." There was a seventh-grade roller-skating party that I told Kelly I would go to even though I knew I couldn't. Besides the fact that it cost money, which I don't have, I don't own Roller Blades anymore and I was not about to rent those dorky skates with four wide wheels.

Brigid whiffed two pitches in a row.

"So what? Just because your grandmother gets sick you can't roller blade?"

There was a loud crack of the bat and I saw Kelly start to move.

"Stay!" I hissed. I leaned right, stretched my arm up and felt the ball smack into my glove. Good old Brigid. I could close my eyes and still catch that ball. I wheeled toward first to make Mrs. Tremont happy, but I couldn't double up Kelly. She was glued to the bag.

"Well," I continued, "my parents had to rush down to her house in Philadelphia, and they told me to stay home and watch Randy." The truth is that I don't even have a grandmother. She died before I was born. But I do love her. I afflict her with all kinds of illnesses whenever I need an excuse for something, and she never complains. She's had everything from brain surgery to a broken foot. She's been in three car accidents and one train wreck. She even got mugged at knifepoint in Philadelphia last week. I was so distraught over that one that Mrs. Miller said I didn't have to take the math test, and she encouraged me to put my head down on my desk and rest.

Kelly looked concerned. "Is she feeling better?"

"Oh, yeah," I said. "She'll be OK."

Gabby snapped on her helmet and stood at the plate. She was a lefty and unpredictable. She struck out half the times she was up, but when she made contact it was usually for extra bases.

"Somebody else was looking for you, too," Kelly sang, "somebody who wanted to skate with you."

I suddenly felt like I'd been hit in the stomach with the ball. "Who?" I managed to ask. I thought I knew, but you have to play dumb in this kind of situation.

"Guess."

"I don't want to."

"You have to. I'm not sure I remember now."

"Don't do a Kellywood on me," I growled. Kelly's in the drama club and she has the most annoying habit of turning a simple story into a giant production, kind of like they do in Hollywood.

Crack! Gabby smacked one. I jumped, but the ball sailed way over my head and up the first base line. Melissa was playing too far over toward center and she had a long run to get to it. If Gabby weren't so slow, she'd have had a home run.

I watched Kelly cross the plate and toss her helmet toward the bench. She winked at me, and then a huge smile spread across her face. I followed her gaze. Three boys emerged from the woods and headed toward the bleachers on the third base side. Great. Just what I needed. I suddenly felt very hot.

IT WAS MY TURN AT BAT. I looked behind me. Randy had halted his bug safari and was standing at the fence watching, his face streaked with dirt.

"Randy, get your fingers out of the fence," I warned.

Mrs. Tremont pitches hard and fast at me. I didn't want any of her wild ones to catch Randy in the knuckles.

I got in my stance. Mrs. Tremont loomed on the mound. She is about six feet tall and as skinny and straight as a flagpole. We could attach our team pennant to the top of her head and she would be so perfectly disguised that no one would be able to find her. She played softball in college and she is good. But not as good as me. She has a windmill delivery that spooks some of the kids, but I concentrate on the ball.

I have always been good at hitting balls, but since last year, I have become even better. Sometimes I feel guilty about my method. When I stand at the plate, I think about my little sister and the secret of what I did that day, and I start to feel a gigantic itch inside me to just smash that ball. I worry that maybe it's a terrible thing to use Rebecca to get a home run. But that day is in my head all the time, and I just bring it to the front when it's my turn at bat. And it feels so good to hit the ball that I want to do it all day long.

Mrs. Tremont went into her windup and threw the first pitch.

"Strike!" she called. But it wasn't. I looked down at Jo. Even through the catcher's mask I could see her rolling her eyes.

The next pitch came in fast, on the outside corner, but I let it go by.

"Strike two," Mrs. Tremont called. "What was wrong with that one?"

"I didn't like it," I said, pawing the ground with my right foot.

"If it's in the strike zone, you better like it, Lindy."

The next pitch was high. I rested the bat on my shoulder. I can be very patient. Mrs. Tremont is always testing me, but I won't chase the bad ones.

Mrs. Tremont threw and I zoned in on the ball. It was coming right down the middle. It was dead. The powerful itch was exploding inside me and I smashed that ball with everything I had. It was out of here. I felt like chasing it down and hitting it again and again. Kristin was playing center field and she didn't even move as it sailed over her head. I jogged around the bases but slowed a bit when I touched third. Eric was standing on the line between me and home plate with his hand outstretched for a high five. It felt weird. I never actually touched his hand before, but I couldn't exactly ignore it. This was only a practice, not a play-off game. It was no big deal. I slapped his hand as I went by. I felt my face getting red, probably from all this practicing in the heat.

"Great hit," he said.

I was past him before I could think of anything to say.

Jo high-fived me at the plate, and when I turned around Eric was back on the bleachers with his friends.

"Water break," Mrs. Tremont called.

Everyone grabbed her water bottle and sat in a circle in the grass on the third base line.

Randy wandered over and crawled into my lap. He looked like Pigpen, that kid from the Charlie Brown cartoon who walks around in a halo of dust.

"You think you could have gotten any dirtier?" I asked.

"He's soooo cute," Kelly sang.

"Want some cookies, Randy?" Gabby leaned forward, offering him her snack pack of mini-Oreos.

My mom never buys cookies, and I felt a little tremor of joy run down Randy's back. Gabby eats too much anyway, so I snagged the bag out of her hand and peeled it open. Randy tried to stuff his fingers in, but I slapped him away.

"Don't you touch it," I said. "There's enough germs on your hands to kill a horse. Even George Washington's horse," I whispered, tickling him under the arm. "Here." I plopped one in his mouth and two in mine.

Brigid was sitting next to me and she ran her hand through Randy's hair. "I would die for those curls," she cooed. "They're so precious!"

Why is it that people always feel the need to touch little kids' curls? If they like the feel, they should just go out and buy themselves a poodle. All my life, no matter where we were, at the playground or in a restaurant, complete strangers would stop and rub their hands over Randy's and Rebecca's heads. No one ever wanted to touch my lifeless, mousy brown hair and that was just fine with me. I wonder if Rebecca's hair is still curly. I wonder if that is a stupid thing for me to wonder about.

"Keep your hands off him!" I finally shouted at Brigid. She was getting on my nerves.

She gave me her "drop dead" look, but I didn't care. I pushed Randy up off my lap. "Go back and play in the dirt."

Randy stumbled to the ground and then sulked off. I finished the cookies while everyone stared at me like I was Attila the Hun. I swear they are all like pampered babies. They live in their big fancy houses and their moms and dads buy them everything they want. They don't know that Randy and I have to be tougher than that. They don't know anything.

"Hey, Lindy!" Greg was on the bleachers holding Eric

by the back of the neck. "Eric wants to talk to you! Come here a minute."

"Oooh, Lindy's got a boyfriend," Kristin chirped. She shoved me in the shoulder.

"Shut up, Kristin."

Kelly winked at me. "I told you so," she said.

"I don't know what you're talking about, Kellywood. Can we just play softball?" I looked around for Mrs. Tremont, but she was yakking away on her cell phone in the parking lot.

"Go on." Now Gabby was shoving my other shoulder.

This is another thing about age twelve that makes no sense at all. All of a sudden, girls are supposed to like those boys that we have hated for the last six years. Boys are OK when they are first born, and they stay kind of normal all the way through kindergarten. Even my old best friend, Andy Carlucci, was a boy. But by second grade, it all changed. The boys started to do disgusting things like turning their eyelids inside out or showing you the wax they just dug out of their ears. They strutted around the playground and tried to make up all the rules for our games. They acted as if they were better than the girls at everything.

Andy and I used to play soccer at recess all the time. But I quit in the middle of second grade because, by then, none of my goals ever counted, and Andy pretended he never saw the out-of-bounds line when his ball crossed over it. He would rather have stood naked in front of the class than get beaten by me in any sport. And I could beat him any day. The girls hated the boys.

Suddenly, now that we are twelve, we are supposed to start liking them again, and I just don't get it.

I got up because I wanted to get away from all the stupid snickering, but I didn't go over to the bleachers. I went and sat on the team bench by myself. I watched Randy pushing a rock down the side of the dirt pile like it was a toy car. I heard a shuffling noise and there was Eric standing next to me.

"Hi," he said. His hands were in his pockets.

I didn't want to be totally rude, so I said "hi" back to him.

"That was an awesome home run you had."

"Thanks." I looked up from the ground. I can't help it, but I do like to look at Eric. He's got this perfect, smooth face with just a few freckles on each cheekbone and shiny brown hair that's always slipping down on his forehead. His blue eyes seem to be always smiling, even when he's just sitting in class staring at the blackboard.

"It was just a practice shot," I added. "No big deal."

"Yeah, well, most kids can't do that — even in practice."

I wondered about Andy Carlucci in Philadelphia. I bet he couldn't do it, either. In a way though it feels weird to brag about something that is as easy as brushing your teeth. So I kept quiet.

"I guess you didn't get to go to the skating party last night."

"No, I couldn't go." I left it at that. I thought I'd give my grandmother a break. She'd already had a rough week.

Eric was moving his feet back and forth in the dirt like he was some kind of horse. What was I supposed to do now? I wished he were a horse so I could pat his back and send him on his way. I played with the laces on my glove.

"I'm having a party," Eric said. "For my birthday."

"Yeah?" Oh, no. I can't believe Kellywood didn't tell me this was coming. I was going to have to afflict my grandmother after all.

Eric put a small white envelope on the bench next to me. It had my name on it. "It would be cool if you could come."

"I don't know . . . " I started. "My grandmother's been . . . "

"She's coming to the party," Kelly butted in. She was leaning up against the fence, eavesdropping on my conversation. "We already talked about it. I hope you don't mind that I told her because, you know, you did mention it to me last night. She said she really wants to go."

I could feel my eyes getting narrow. If I didn't shut Kelly up, she'd have me in love and getting married by next week. But Eric beat me to it.

"Great," he said. "It's gonna be a good party. I'll see ya." And he took off.

I threw my glove on the ground. "Kelly, I can't believe you did that!"

"Did what? What's the big deal? It's just a party. Why can't you go?"

"Well, my grandmother's been sick and . . . "

"You just said that she was going to be fine. You're just scared to go."

I grabbed my glove and stalked off onto the field. Kelly was right. I was sort of scared. But not the way she thought. These kids in Shelbourne probably wore real nice clothes to their parties and brought expensive presents. Most of my clothes come from the thrift shop and some were leftover donations from That Place we used to live. I will be like Cinderella going to the ball without any fashion help from the Fairy Godmother. And I'm not even close to being pretty. Somebody will nail me for sure, probably Melissa Weatherfield.

I threw a few high pop-ups to myself, taking comfort in the feel of the ball smacking into the leather. It's kind of weird. I do sort of want to go to the party anyway. I swear I must have a death wish. I put my hand over my back pocket and felt the invitation. I haven't had one of those in a long time. I wondered if he wrote it out himself.

Mrs. Tremont made us line up in two straight rows and practice throwing the ball back and forth to each other while she did some paperwork. Melissa was across from me. She's got a decent arm, but nothing special.

She tossed me the ball. "Hey, guys," she blurted, "you know that weird mannequin head that's right by the bypass?"

"Yeah. It's really strange," Jo called. "My mom insists that the cops have radar in it. She got a ticket near there a couple of weeks ago."

My hands were sweaty and I lost my grip on the ball. It flew over Melissa's head and she had to run to get it.

"There's no radar in it!" Melissa laughed, jogging back to her place. "You know how you can see a couple of shelves, like steps, on it?"

"Yeah." Gabby tossed her ball to Jo. "There's

always different stuff on there. Like one time there were oranges and one time old sneakers."

Sweat was breaking out on my forehead and my stomach was so heavy it felt like all those old sneakers were piled up down there.

"Did you guys hear that the Phillies swept the Braves?" I shouted. "First time in over twenty-five years."

They ignored me.

"Well," Melissa prattled on. "I know who put that thing up."

I froze. Melissa threw the ball. It thudded in the grass next to me.

"Who?" everyone asked.

"It's that trash-picker guy. He must live in there somewhere. I always wondered where he came from. I know it's him because I cleaned my room last week and threw out some of my old stuffed animals. And wouldn't you know, next time I ride by on the bypass, there's my old kitty hanging out on the top shelf."

I was aiming at Melissa's head when I threw, but she was laughing so hard that she fell on the ground and the ball sailed way past her. Jo was doubled over laughing, too, and I could see a big smile spreading across Kelly's face.

"No way!" Gabby cried.

"It's true!" Melissa insisted.

I saw Randy, face pressed up against the fence. He was staring at me, his mouth half-open.

"He is one freaky guy." Melissa recovered long enough to throw the ball back to me. "I think the police should arrest him or something. Where does he live anyway, in some shack by the highway? I bet he's an escaped murderer."

I felt a giant iceberg growing inside me. And that itch was back, bigger than anytime I had ever stood at the plate. I saw Randy run off and hide under the bleachers. I wound up. I admit my aim was off. I was trying to get it in her big, fat mouth. If she was paying attention, she could have caught it. But she didn't. I smacked that softball into Melissa's chest at about sixty miles per hour, and she dropped to the ground like she was shot. She moaned and rolled over, her face in the dirt. Everyone froze for a minute, staring, then ran to hover over her twitching body. But not me. I was glad.

5

◆ ◆ ◆

I GRABBED RANDY BY THE HAND and headed across the fields toward home. I heard Mrs. Tremont calling my name, but I ignored her. Kelly came puffing up behind me and grabbed my shoulder. She looked at me like I had four eyes.

"Lindy," she blurted. "Mrs. Tremont says that if you don't come back right now, you are definitely, positively, officially off the team! She wants to talk to you."

I stopped walking. I knew she wouldn't throw me off the team for being late. But maybe she would for trying to kill the right fielder. I have to play softball. It's the only thing from my old life that I've got left. It's the only thing in this whole world that I am good at. It's the only thing that keeps me from being a total leper at Mecong Middle School.

"I'll wait here," I said. I sat in the tall grass beyond right field with Randy in my lap. "But I'm not coming back."

I ran my fingers through Randy's hair and watched the girls leave the field one by one as their parents came to pick them up. I saw Melissa give me a long, cold look before she got into her big SUV and roared off with her rich lawyer father. She'll probably sue me, but I don't care. I wish I had hit her harder.

Mrs. Tremont stood alone on the mound and stared at me, but I wasn't about to go crawling back. I sat in the field, quiet as a bug, and let her come out to me. She walked real slow, glaring at me the whole time. She thinks she can scare me, but she can't.

"Lindy. Stand up. I'm going to give you and your brother a ride home."

"We can walk," I said.

"I know you can walk. But today you are going to ride home with me."

My mind was racing. "I'm not allowed to ride with strangers," I insisted.

"Now." Mrs. Tremont pointed her four-foot arm toward the parking lot. "Or else your softball career is over. And I mean it this time."

"C'mon, Randy." I held his hand and walked toward her little car. He had tear streaks running through the dirt on his face. I wondered if Melissa had made him cry or whether it was me.

Mrs. Tremont unlocked the door and I buckled Randy into the back seat. There were papers everywhere.

Mrs. Tremont is an English teacher, and I guess that she uses her car as a filing cabinet. I moved aside a bunch of tests and sat next to Randy.

"You can sit up front here," Mrs. Tremont said.

"But that's the most dangerous seat in the car, Mrs. Tremont. And I hope you don't mind me saying this, but your car doesn't look like the kind that comes equipped with passenger-side air bags. I'd feel a lot safer back here." And I did, too.

Mrs. Tremont sighed and started the engine. She glanced at me in the rearview mirror, and I could see she was gathering her thoughts for the big lecture. I decided to fire first.

"Do you get paid for coaching, Mrs. Tremont?" I asked.

She hesitated. "Well, yes. The district gives coaches a little something extra. Why?"

"I was just wondering," I said. "Because I know you get paid for teaching, and if you mark papers while you're coaching, it's sort of like getting paid double for one job. Not that I mind, of course. It's just that I wouldn't want you to get in any trouble." I said it real sweet-like, but I wanted her to know that I had something on her. Maybe it would make her think twice about turning me in.

Her eyebrows went up, but she didn't say anything.

I think she got the point.

"Which way, Lindy?" Mrs. Tremont asked.

We were at the end of the parking lot. "Oh, this is close enough," I said. "We can walk from here." I tried to open my door, but it was locked.

Mrs. Tremont put the car in park and turned around in her seat. "Lindy, if I have to, I will go into the school and get your file and find your address. Now which way should I turn?"

"I was just trying to save you some trouble, that's all. Go left. I live in the River Meadows development. Do you know where that is? It's a really pretty place, but it has a stupid name. There aren't any rivers or meadows. Who thinks of these names anyway?" I figured the more I talked, the less Mrs. Tremont could. I took a quick breath and rambled on. "I've been to Pony Chase, Fox Run, and Swan Pointe, and I've never seen one pony, fox, or swan in any of them. I think they ought to call the developments Alcatraz One, Alcatraz Two, and so on. Alcatraz is a prison, in case you didn't know."

"I know," Mrs. Tremont interrupted. "And just why are the developments in Shelbourne like prisons?"

It was working. I definitely had her distracted. Only problem was, Randy was crying again, his chin all the way down on his chest. Maybe it was the prison word. I quick reached over and dried his face with the bottom of his T-shirt. I did it kind of rough and he got the message.

"Well, Mrs. Tremont," I continued, "it's not like a prison for you and the rest of the adults who have cars, but it is for kids. There's nothing here but a bunch of houses — no movies, no stores, no nothing. And every development is surrounded by highways. You try to escape and — bam! — you get squished. Cities make much more sense. They've got sidewalks and buses and you can walk lots of places."

"Is that where you used to live, in the city?" Mrs. Tremont was turning into River Meadows.

"Oh no, of course not," I quickly added. "It's just that I've heard about cities from my grandmother. She's lived in a lot of places."

Suburban people think that kids from the city are all thugs and thieves. Mrs. Tremont already had a low opinion of me. I didn't want to add to it. "Go right at the stop sign," I said.

Mrs. Tremont drove slowly, staring at the houses.

"Our place is just up around the curve," I said, "on the left. It's number 34." I had my hand on Randy's leg, ready to pinch him real hard if he started to contradict me.

Mrs. Tremont pulled into the driveway. This was the McCallisters' house. It looked like a castle, all stone in the front with two big peaks on either side. You could look right into the foyer and see a giant chandelier hanging there. I swear, at night that chandelier sends out enough light that it could guide the space shuttle in for a landing.

I saw Randy's mouth begin to open, so I gave him a little pinch just for good measure. I pulled at the lock and jumped out real fast, dragging my brother behind me. He had a Big Mac wrapper stuck to his leg. I threw it back into the car. "Thanks for the ride," I called and headed straight for the backyard.

"Lindy! Wait!"

I pretended I didn't hear her. Randy and I slid into the yard, and I latched the gate behind us. I didn't have any breakfast this morning and there was a giant emptiness growing in the pit of my stomach. But my mind was working fast anyway. It had to.

There was just no way I was going to let Mrs. Tremont see my real house. What if my father was home? What if she started asking questions? I picked the McCallisters' as my pretend home because they don't have any kids, and they work a lot. They call me sometimes when they're out late and ask me if I would walk Missy, their miniature collie. I know where the key is. I know how to get into their house. I said a real quick prayer that they weren't home. Lying can take you only so far. You need some luck, too.

"Why can't she just go away and mind her own business?" I whispered. I was peeking through the slat in the fence. Randy was pressed up against the wall of the house like he was just waiting for the firing squad to fill him with holes.

Mrs. Tremont turned the engine off. That was a bad sign. "C'mon, Gumby." I grabbed Randy's stiff little body and pulled him onto the deck. I bent his legs and sat him on the top step. "Stay right there. I'll be back in a minute."

"Lindy!" he hissed.

I whirled around. "What?"

"This isn't our house."

"You're kidding!" I smacked my hand against my forehead. "I must've accidentally come to the wrong place. It looks just like our house! Anybody could get confused." I gazed around the yard at the swimming pool, the flower garden, the cutesy little statues and birdbaths. So boring. No armor on the trees, no flagpoles with mannequin heads.

Randy's whole body was shaking. "What if the police come?" he whimpered.

I really didn't have time for this. "For the one-billionth time, the police are not coming!"

"Can I come with you? Please?" His little hands were gripped together. I was worried he was going to wet his pants. "I don't want to stay by myself."

But I couldn't let him come. I had too much lying to do in there and Randy is hopeless, even as a silent accomplice. "No. You stay there. And don't you move."

I tilted the flowerpot, grabbed the key, and unlocked the back door. I stuck my head inside. "Mrs. McCallister? Helloooo? Anybody home?" My voice bounced off the walls. Missy padded up to me, her paws clicking against the marble kitchen floor. I knelt down and scratched her behind the ears. This dog reminds me of Randy sometimes, all quiet and trembly and no bark at all.

The doorbell rang. Missy looked up, but I held her collar. "Not yet, girl. Let's make her wait a bit."

After the third ring, I finally went and opened the front door. "Mrs. Tremont! You're back! I guess I forgot to give you the directions for getting home. All you have to do is . . . "

"I don't need directions, Lindy. I'd like to talk to your parents for a minute." She stepped right inside without being invited as if she were afraid I was going to slam the door on her. I admit, I was thinking about it.

I picked Missy up. "Sorry, but they're not home." I wished this dog would bite, or maybe just growl a little. I leaned on the door with my hand on the knob. I gave Mrs. Tremont my sweetest smile. "I'll be sure to tell them you said 'hi.'" That was her cue to leave.

But she didn't take it. She just kept standing there, her eyes taking in everything—the fancy living room that no one ever lived in, the big dining room with the tall china closet. Before I came here, I swear I used to think that a china closet was someplace that you kept your Chinese things. But it's not. It's a cabinet that's got lots of dishes in it that you don't use for eating, just for showing.

Mrs. Tremont crossed her arms and craned her skinny neck to look past me down the hall. She pushed her small glasses back up above the bony bump on her nose. She stared at me with her little watery eyes. We both knew that neither one of us belonged here, but she was too chicken to accuse me. She couldn't figure out how I got inside. I hate to brag, but I am so good. I almost felt sorry for Mrs. Tremont, standing there with her face all screwed up, the words stuck like too much peanut butter in her throat. But I got over it real fast. There was no telling when the McCallisters might come back. My luck couldn't hold out forever.

I yawned real loud. "It was nice of you to stop by," I said in my most formal voice. "But I have to go and fix some lunch for Randy. Saturday is the maid's day off." I almost bust out laughing at the look on Mrs. Tremont's face.

"Yes . . . well . . . fine," Mrs. Tremont stumbled. She took a step back, crossed her arms, and stared at me with her squinty eyes. "I'm sure I can arrange to stop by again. I'm very much looking forward to meeting your parents." She said it nice-like, but I knew it was a threat.

I gave her one of my fake smiles, then slammed the door after she left. Good riddance. She never even got the chance to lecture me about hitting Melissa.

"C'mon, Randy," I said, locking the back door and hiding the key in its place. "Let's get home."

We took a shortcut through some backyards and squeezed through a hole in the shrubbery onto our property. Mom was sitting in the rocking chair on the porch, her arms crossed. I got that sinking feeling that I must have forgotten to do something. Again.

RANDY DASHED UP THE STEPS and crawled onto Mom's lap. She started to rock him and he stuck his thumb in his mouth, dirt and all. I turned away. I leaned up against the rail and stared out at the tops of the shrubs. Mom was quiet, but I could tell that she was worked up about something by the way that rocking chair was crack-cracking against the uneven porch.

"Were you at softball practice?" she finally asked.

"Uh-huh." It's a good thing my back was turned because I could not help rolling my eyes. Since my driver's license has not yet been approved and my personal limousine driver has the day off, where else could I possibly go? I thumped my glove down on the porch to emphasize the stupidity of that question. But I don't know if my mother got the point.

Why is it that grown-ups are always asking you questions that they already know the answers to? My mother is an expert at this. At least three times a week she says, "Lindy, have you done your homework yet?" when she knows for a fact that I have not even brought my backpack into the house. When I answer her back a little too sharply, she asks, "How would you like to skip dinner and spend the rest of the night in your room?"

But my mother has never asked me a single question about Rebecca. Sometimes I wish she would at least ask. I know why she doesn't. She thinks she knows everything that happened. She's always trying to get me to talk about what I feel, but she doesn't know to ask me what I did. I don't think I could tell her the truth anyway. Maybe I could if she asked. Maybe it wouldn't hurt so much if I got it all out, confessed everything. But maybe it would hurt more.

I picked at the splinters on the railing.

"I like to know where you and Randy are, Lindy. I hate to be sitting here worrying like this. How many times have I told you that you're supposed to leave me a note on the refrigerator when you go out?"

This was another question that I could not answer since I do not exactly keep a tally sheet of motherly instructions in my pocket. Even if I tried, my pants would bulge fatter than Principal Travis's backside. Since I didn't have an answer, I said nothing. But it wasn't fair. I take good care of Randy.

That rocker was creak-creakin', faster and faster, and I took a quick peek to make sure she wasn't rocking clear across the porch. Sometimes I worry that she's going to wear a hole right through those old wooden planks and disappear under the house, chair and all. Lots of nights, when I can't sleep, I lie in bed and listen to the slow, steady squeak of that rocker. And I know that she's sitting out here all alone, pushing herself back and forth, just staring out at the darkness. Right now, though, she was staring straight at me and her forehead was still all wrinkled up with the worry that something had happened to Randy and me.

I could have defended myself, I guess, and explained how obvious it was that I was at softball practice, but I didn't want to. I felt around on the rail for one of those big splinters and jammed it into my finger. "Owww!" I screamed, only half-faking because it did hurt. I grabbed my hand and cradled it to my chest. I bit hard on my lower lip.

My mother stopped rocking, her feet flat on the porch, and even Randy lifted his head to look at me. "What happened?!" she asked.

I squeezed my finger real hard to force out a drop of blood. "Look," I said, sniffling. "I got a splinter."

"Oh, baby." My mom stood up. She put Randy down onto the porch and peeled his hands off her shirt. "Let me see."

I rested my head on her shoulder. "It's a big one," she said, her small, smooth hands cupped around my injured one. "But that'll make it easy to get out. Hold on." She yanked the splinter and I winced.

"I think I got it all, sweetie," Mom said. "But we should put a Band-Aid on it to keep an infection out."

She went in the house and Randy followed her like a shadow. She came back without him and I wondered how she managed to shake him off.

"Let me see," she said.

I held out my hand and she gave my finger a shot of first-aid spray. She was still in her hospital uniform and I swear, with a little better hairstyle and some of the make-up that she used to wear, people would think she was a doctor. She never got past the eleventh grade, but she knows tons of stuff about making people feel better. She would never have acted like that stupid doctor who came to our house that day last year. I was only eleven then, but I could see right away what he thought when he looked at Dad, his lips pressed together real tight. It's no wonder that Dad won't go see a doctor now, even with all Mom's pleading.

It's not true what the doctor thought. Only I know who's to blame, and I haven't told anyone. I bit down hard on the inside of my cheek and sucked on the cut that I had opened up. I'm not psycho or anything. It's just that it feels kind of good sometimes to taste that salty, warm blood on my tongue and to think about nothing except for the pain traveling up the side of my head.

Mom finished putting the Band-Aid on my finger. "Where's Dad?" she asked.

I shrugged. "He was in the yard this morning, working on something." I wished he were on his way back to Philadelphia. Sometimes I think that his real self is still in the city, floating around somewhere, and his body is lost here in Shelbourne. If only they could meet up, they could get back together again. Maybe I could find a place to buy a map and figure out the best way for us to walk.

Our eyes trailed over the patchy lawn. There were rusty pipes, pieces of chain, old bicycle tires, a small broken television, a child's radio, and the beginning of a new, strange sculpture.

She stood for a moment, sucking on her lower lip. She rested her arm on my shoulder. "Well, let's go in," she finally said. "You'll fix Randy something to eat, won't you? I'm beat." She didn't wait for an answer. She went straight upstairs.

When kids ask me what my mom does, I tell them that she is the single-most talented doctor in the entire hospital and that she gets assigned to all the most complicated medical cases. She saved at least ten lives just last month. But I do worry that sooner or later some kid from school will see her pushing a broom down the halls of Mercy Medical or emptying those disgusting trash cans. I pray for the health of my classmates every single night before I go to bed.

Randy was sprawled on the floor, working on one of those 3-D puzzles. He is a puzzle genius, but I still think it would be better if he played baseball. I opened every darn cabinet in the kitchen, and all I found was a half a loaf of bread, a box of Fruit Loops, and some cheese crackers. We were totally out of milk, and there wasn't enough peanut butter left to spread on one cracker, let alone make two sandwiches. My stomach started to growl and I felt my teeth clench together real hard. I knew just who was to blame.

"Freddy!" I called. He didn't answer me, so I kicked the couch a few times. Freddy is so worthless that even the evil couch doesn't want him and never sucks him in. He was lying there in a T-shirt and gym shorts with his eyes half-closed.

"Freddy!" I hit him with a pillow. He made a low moaning sound. It was the only way I could tell that he was actually alive. "Did you bring home anything to eat last night?"

He rolled over a bit. "I forgot," he mumbled.

"You forgot?! That's just great. Thanks a lot. Now what are we going to eat for lunch?" I walked around the couch, kicking it every few steps. "How could you forget? You work right in the stupid store."

Freddy is sixteen and he has a part-time job in Eckles, one of those giant drug stores that sells everything from cough drops to bicycles. Mom's always asking him to bring stuff home, and he never does it. She says that he forgets because his mind's on girls. I think he forgets because he doesn't have a mind.

I stopped kicking the couch because it didn't seem to be bothering Freddy any and I was getting weak with hunger.

I stared at the stuff on the kitchen table. "Hey, Randy," I called. "Come here. I got a real big surprise. We're going to have a special lunch, and you get to help make it."

Randy hopped up into a chair.

"It's a brand-new invention, and you are the very first one to try it." I put two pieces of bread in front of him and I poured some Fruit Loops onto the table.

Randy looked up at me kind of weird.

"Fruit Loop sandwiches," I announced. "But you can't just pour them on any way you want. Oh no. If you want to do it the proper way, you have to make a pattern. Watch." I put the purples all around the edges by the crust and then started a row of green. "Can you do it?"

Randy nodded, kind of excited-like, and started picking out the reds and yellows from the pile and squashing them into his bread. His hands were still filthy, but I figured since he already ate about a pound of dirt today, a few more sprinkles wouldn't kill him. Besides, I just wasn't in the mood to yell at him.

The phone rang and I grabbed it real quick so it wouldn't wake Mom. "Hello?" I mumbled through a mouthful of Fruit Loops.

"Lindy?"

I almost gagged. A piece of dry cereal was stuck in my throat. I couldn't get any words out.

"Lindy, I would like to speak to one of your parents for a minute." Mrs. Tremont sure was persistent. "Put your mother or father on the phone right now, please."

She was going to have to try a lot harder than that.

"I'm sorry," I squeaked, the Fruit Loop still lodged partially in my windpipe. "You must have the wrong number."

I hung up, waited a few seconds, then took the phone off the hook. My mother needed her sleep.

"Beautiful work, Chef Randy," I said, returning to the table with a sigh. His bread had turned into a colorful masterpiece. "Now, let's eat!"

We put the tops on the sandwiches and picked them up. I forgot that Fruit Loops aren't quite as sticky as peanut butter. About half of our sandwich stuffing fell out and started jumping across the table and rolling onto the floor.

"Don't worry about them," I said. "Eat up." And it wasn't so bad — weird and crunchy, but kind of tasty. Maybe I'll invent Fruit Loop soup for dinner.

"What's that?" Freddy had dragged himself off the couch and stood, in his usual slouch, beside the kitchen table.

I threw a handful of cereal at him. "Fruit Loop sandwiches," I spat. "What else could we eat since you didn't bring home any peanut butter or milk or anything?"

Freddy shrugged. He pulled a piece of bread from the bag and made a tic-tac-toe board on it with the Fruit Loops. "Wanna play, big guy?" he asked Randy.

They played three games and he let Randy win every time, which is a big mistake in my opinion. Losing is a fact of life. It's another one of those bricks that Randy needs to learn how to catch.

Freddy ate the game board after each one of his losses, which made Randy giggle. It made me sick because Freddy always eats with his mouth wide open like a big, old horse. It's disgusting.

Freddy has about one thousand friends, and hard as I try, I cannot figure out what they like about him. He is one of the most annoying people on this planet. The only things he ever does are listen to music and lie on the couch. I hate to admit it, but he looks just like me, and that is no compliment. But at least I comb my hair. Freddy gets invited to parties almost every weekend. It is the only thing that gets him off the couch.

"Hey, Freddy," I said, slowly pulling Eric's invitation from my back pocket and fingering it under the table.

He looked up and wiped the sugar crumbs onto his shirt. I tried not to look too disgusted. "You know those parties you go to?" I asked.

"Yeah?" He leaned on his elbows and stared at me through his messy hair.

"Well, I was just sort of wondering, are any of them birthday parties?"

"Uh-huh. Some."

"Do you bring, like, presents or something?"

The edges of Freddy's lips curled up, and he looked at Randy. "Oooh, Belinda must be invited to a party."

I jumped up so fast I knocked my chair to the floor. He knows how much I hate that name. I tried to whack him in the head, but he caught my arm on the way down.

"Money or CDs," he said while I struggled to get free of his grasp. "Something like that."

"I don't care," I screamed at him. "I'm not going to any stupid party anyway. Let go!" I pulled loose and stormed out onto the porch.

That's when I first saw what Dad brought home.

I FROZE ON THE PORCH, and he looked up at me from the yard. "Lindy, would you get me a brush?" He was on his knees.

I felt sick, like I had eaten something real bad and it was lying heavy in the bottom of my stomach. The screen door clicked and Randy was standing beside me, his mouth hanging open.

"Randy, get me a brush, OK?" Dad asked.

Randy ran in the house, and I was sure that he was going to go hide in his room. But I was wrong. He came back out with the brush.

Freddy was there, too, and he gave me a quick sideways look before going down to Dad. For a moment I forgot how worthless Freddy is and I thought for sure he would do something. But he just stood there, looking.

A big truck rumbled by and I felt the porch vibrate. The gravel thrown up by its wheels pinged against the fence. Dad started brushing.

I guess I was going to have to take care of it myself. I wanted to scream at them, but I kept real good control of myself. "It's dead, Dad," I said. "You should go put it back where you got it." I was holding onto the rail real tight and I didn't even care if I got another splinter.

"I know it's dead, Lindy." Dad paused for a minute to answer me. "I'm just taking care of it, that's all. I couldn't leave it out there on the road." He was brushing out the tangled, matted hair of the lifeless cat, its little legs crossed carefully in front of him.

"You shouldn't have brought it home," I said, my voice rising. "You can't take care of it. It's already dead."

"I know it's dead, Lindy." He was talking to me like I was the crazy one. My dad always used to feed half-dead cats and romp in the park with strangers' dogs. He even rescued spiders from Mom's broom, catching them in his hands and carrying them outside. One time he bottle-fed an orphaned baby squirrel for weeks until it was big enough to be set free. But this was the first time he ever brought home something that was 100 percent dead. If it wasn't so disgusting, I would have gone down there and gotten rid of it myself.

"Just put it over the fence!" I stamped my foot. "Pleeeeease!"

Dad just shook his head. Even Randy was petting that cat's head. I couldn't believe him. "Randy," I screamed, "that cat is dead. Don't you touch it. It could have rabies or fleas or something." I turned my attention to Freddy. "Are you just going to stand there?"

Freddy walked over to the shed and brought out a spade. He started to dig a hole near the hubcap tree.

"Fine," I shouted at them. "This is just fine." Not only do we have a mannequin-head flagpole and a trash sculpture garden, but now we will have a dead cat buried under the hubcap tree.

I guess I was being a little too loud because the screen door clicked again and there was Mom, her hair messier than ever and dark circles hanging like half-moons under her eyes. I know I should have felt guilty about waking her up. But I didn't. I was glad she was here.

"Look!" I panted. "Look at what they're doing!" I crossed my arms on my chest, confident that Mom would take control and clear that dead cat out of here.

She put her hand on my shoulder for a second, squeezing, then pulled her sweater close and walked down into the yard. Randy and Dad looked up at her. Freddy paused, leaning on the spade.

"It's a cat," Randy whispered. "Wanna see?"

Mom bent low and Randy took her hand, guiding it over the soft fur, down toward the tail. She looked up at Dad. He was kneeling but leaning back on his old work boots, his hands resting on his worn jeans.

"I couldn't leave it there, Tess," he explained, "with no one to . . ." His voice trailed off.

Mom put her hand on Dad's for a moment and then nodded. "I know you couldn't," she said. She just crouched there and watched him brush.

My whole family had gone completely crazy. "You're gonna agree with them?!" I threw my hands up in the air. "That is just great. Terrific. What's going to happen when a deer gets hit out there? Huh? Did you think of that?"

Freddy started digging again and it felt as though hundreds of crawly things were stuck under my skin, running all around. Mom stood up and pulled Randy with her, resting him on her hip.

"He's going to suck his thumb now!" I exploded. "Then he's going to get cat germs and then who knows what! And you're doing nothing about it!"

Mom came up onto the porch and put her arm through mine, but I pulled away. "Freddy's going to take care of it, Lindy," she said. "Come on inside and sit with me."

"No, thanks." I ran into the house and straight up to my room, slamming the door. I kicked the clothes around the floor for a while, and then I leaned on the windowsill and watched for those big, flat-topped tractor-trailers. I counted how many seconds it took them to round the bend and pass this house. I practiced jumping by leaping from my bed to the closet. There was a knock on my door.

"Lindy? Are you OK?" My mom was rattling the doorknob. But I had the lock on.

"I'm fine, fine, fine," I sang.

"Lindy, let me in for a minute. Can't we talk?"

"No." Even though she said "please" four times, I just lay quietly on my bed, staring at the ceiling. She finally gave up, and before long I heard the rhythmic creaking of the rocking chair on the porch.

Sometimes I just can't believe how strange my family has become. When I lived in Philadelphia we were normal, even cool, and I used to make fun of the weird families on our block. There was old Mrs. Kaiser, who lived on the corner and fed the squirrels. Those little rats would actually come scratching at her screen door, and she would sit on her front stoop with big curlers in her hair and throw nuts to them. She had two big buckteeth and I used to tell everybody that she was part squirrel herself.

And there was the Groblinka family. They came from some country I never heard of and they couldn't speak English too well. Their kids wore weird clothes and always had snot running out of their noses as if they didn't know that tissues had been invented. I put a box of Kleenex with a little bow around it by their front door one day, just to give them a hint about the modern world.

I can only imagine what I'd find at my front door if the kids at Mecong ever found out about my family. I went back to the window and counted the seconds as the big trucks came around the bend.

Sometimes I think that Rebecca is the lucky one.

I wonder where she is. I wonder if she hates me.

MONDAY MORNINGS ARE THE WORST. I sat in homeroom slumped in my desk, my head resting on a pile of books, while Mrs. Terwinsky, our vice-principal, droned on and on with the morning announcements over the loudspeaker. This is usually a good time to flip paper clips at your enemies, but I was too tired.

Kelly nudged my arm. "Lindy, did you do that math homework?"

I bolted up in my seat. "No. Of course I didn't. What a stupid question." I always copy Kelly's homework at lunch. "Didn't you?"

"I forgot to bring my book home over the weekend. I was hoping you had done it."

"Oh, great," I moaned. "How could you forget your book?! What is the matter with you?" I let my head flop back down on my desk.

"We could do some now and finish up at lunch," Kelly suggested. "We can get it done before class."

I do like Kelly, but sometimes I think she is way too cheerful for me. She took out one of her perfectly sharpened pencils and started writing in her notebook. I watched her with my one open eye. "Do you iron your notebook pages?" I asked. I swear, no one has more perfect books than Kelly. Even the edges of her pages don't curl.

Kelly gave me a half smile. "What's the matter with you today?"

"Your cheerfulness is making me ill," I said.

"You look tired. You should go to bed earlier. I make sure I get at least eight hours of sleep each night. I just don't feel right if I don't."

"Well, Miss Perfect, for your information, I did go to bed early. I just have dreams sometimes that wake me up." I don't think Kelly would sleep too well, either, if she had a dead cat buried in her backyard.

"Really?" Kelly turned completely around in her seat, and her freckled face was lit up with curiosity. "What are they about? I read this article in a magazine a couple of weeks ago about interpreting dreams. I could help you! First, you have to figure out what . . . "

"Forget it!" I interrupted. "Forget I said anything." I squeezed my eyes shut. I'd rather introduce Kelly to the hubcap tree than to my dream. It isn't exactly hard to interpret. There are no mysterious symbols or weird floating aliens or anything. It's just Rebecca. She's looking up at me with those little baby eyes and she's holding her arms out. I want to pick her up, but no matter how hard I try, I can't reach her. And then she slips away, underneath the bubbles. I have this dream all the time.

A lump was rising in my throat. I chewed on the inside of my cheek and ran my tongue over the warm oozing blood. I never knew that just two minutes could change a person's life forever. Now that I know, I am always on the lookout. You just never know when another two minutes might come along and change your life again. It makes me so mad that I can't have them back. I think I should be allowed to do them over, like the math quiz that I messed up a few weeks ago. I know for sure that I would get those two minutes right the second time around.

Kelly was poking my arm. "Are you listening to me? Come on," she whined.

"Yeah, come on," mimicked Derrick Pierce. "We want to hear about your big bad dream."

Derrick sits in front of me. He's my favorite target when shooting paper clips. My all-time best shot ringed a piece of his bleach-blond spiked hair. If I were in a competition, it would have been worth a thousand points at least. That paper clip hung there half the day before he noticed. It kind of fit in with all his other weird jewelry anyway.

"Shut up, bleach head," I said. "Why don't you go pop a few pimples or something and leave me alone?"

Derrick smirked at me. I swear he's got the biggest nostrils of any person I ever met. "I bet Lindy's nightmare is that Eric the Wonder Boy discovers what a loser she really is and drops her."

I sat up. "I'm not going out with Eric. Who told you that?" I glanced over at Kelly. She just shrugged, but her face was turning red. I swear, someday I'm going to have to superglue her lips together.

Derrick started making kissing noises. He doesn't exactly have the quietest voice in the world either, and other kids were turning around to look at us. I had enough. With my hands under my desk I unfolded one of those big paper clips, and aiming for a piece of bare skin between his pants and his shirt, I jammed that paper clip as hard as I could into Derrick's lower back. He jumped so hard that his whole desk came up off the floor with him and then crashed back down again. He was holding his back and making some noises, but they sure weren't kissing noises. I shut him up good.

"Mr. Pierce?" Mr. Strykus, our homeroom teacher, lowered his newspaper and stared down the aisle. "Are you having a problem you would like to share with the class?"

And then Derrick did it. I can't believe he did it, but he screamed the bad word and he followed it right up with my name. I think he might even have hit me if Mr. Strykus hadn't jumped out of his desk and grabbed him by the back of his shirt. I might have enjoyed the whole thing except that Mr. Strykus sent us both down to the counselor's office.

My week was sure starting off great. "Hey, Derrick," I said as we walked down the hall, "did you have a birthday party last year?"

"What?" He looked at me like I had fifteen eyes.

It's just that Eric's party was this weekend and I was getting desperate for a good idea for a present. "Oh, never mind," I said to Derrick. He wouldn't be any help anyway. He probably got nose rings and bleach for his birthday. Eric wasn't into that stuff.

Derrick stalked off and I didn't try to keep up with him. He had a little red mark on the back of his shirt and I guess I must have accidentally hit a vein or something. I was only trying to get him to shut up. If he had just minded his own business, none of this would have ever happened. It wasn't my fault.

When I got to the little waiting room I sat down right beside him to show that there were no hard feelings, but he got up and moved away. I guess he was going to rat me out.

"Hey, Derrick," I said. "Did you know I have a cousin who lives in Philadelphia?"

Derrick used the bad word on me again.

"The kids in Philadelphia are really tough. My cousin said that one time this kid named Billy McKenzie practically choked Andy Carlucci to death at recess. When they got back in the classroom, Andy's neck still had big red handprints on it. When the teacher asked Andy how it happened, he stood up in front of the whole class and told everybody that he had choked himself because he was having a bad day. That Andy was sure tough."

Mr. Dalton swung his door open and gave Derrick and me the stare. He called Derrick first. Derrick shuffled into the office without even looking back at me, and the door closed with an ominous click. Great. I wished I had those magical red shoes like Dorothy in *The Wizard of Oz.* I could just click my heels together and say, "There's no place like Philadelphia. There's no place like Philadelphia." Kids know how to stick together in Philadelphia. I swear, they do.

MR. DALTON POINTED to a hard wooden chair in front of his desk and I sat down. Before he could open his mouth, though, there was a knock at the door.

"Yes?"

Mrs. Mastopolis, the secretary, popped her head in the room. "It's Mrs. Brighton," she said, "on line one."

Mr. Dalton looked down at the blinking button on the telephone, then he looked at me. "I'll take it out there," he said. "Tell her I'll be right with her." He closed up my student folder and left the room.

I didn't know who Mrs. Brighton was, but I sure hoped she was a windbag. I grabbed the folder off Mr. Dalton's desk and flipped it open. Belinda Perkins, it said at the top. I felt the familiar snarl creep across my face when I saw that name. I swiped a black felt pen from the blotter. I might never get another chance like this to alter my permanent record. I quickly scratched out Belinda and replaced it with Lindy in my neatest handwriting. I will never forgive my mother for giving me that name. She got it off of some television show she liked. Frederick, Belinda, and Randolph. You would have thought we were from some royal family or something, with our noses stuck up in the air. Rebecca got the best name of all. At least she got that. I wonder if she still uses it or if she has a different name now.

I could hear Mr. Dalton's droning voice on the other side of the door. I flipped past my registration form to my old school records. This was even more important than altering my name. I had to make a quick decision. I thought about ripping out the pages from Franklin Elementary in Leedstown, but then he would probably notice the gap in my schooling. I was only there a few months, but I don't want to have to do any part of seventh grade over again. I read real fast, looking to see if they had my old address down there anywhere. They did. It was 1311 Bradley Boulevard, Leedstown, Pennsylvania. I didn't know if Mr. Dalton was familiar with the address of the homeless shelter, but I wasn't taking any chances. It was bad enough having the kids at Franklin Elementary know about it. At least there, I wasn't the only one. And besides, the kids at Franklin didn't live in dinosaur houses and take Christmas vacations in Europe.

I carefully crossed out Bradley Boulevard and had just started to write in Violet Lane when I noticed that it had gotten awfully quiet. Just in time, I heard the doorknob turn. I flung the folder back onto Mr. Dalton's desk. It wasn't until the last second as that folder went skidding across the desk that I saw the coffee mug. I lunged for it just as the door opened, but I was too late. I couldn't have had a more direct hit if I was trying. The mug flew off the edge of the desk and crashed to the floor, and that coffee shot up in the air like it was coming out of a volcano.

This day was just getting better all the time. I turned around real slowly. Mr. Dalton didn't say a word. He was gripping the door, and his chin was hanging down all the way to his tie. If he didn't shut his mouth soon, there was going to be a pool of drool on the floor to mix with that coffee.

"Mr. Dalton," I said to break him out of his trance. "You shouldn't keep your coffee mug so close to the edge of your desk. When you barged in here, the whole room just shook. I thought we were having an earthquake. I tried to catch that mug, but I couldn't. I'll clean it up, though. I don't mind helping out. I'm a very helpful kind of person." I started picking up the broken pieces of the mug. It was an ugly one anyway. Looked like it was probably twenty years old.

"Sally," Mr. Dalton called into the waiting area, "could you grab me a roll of paper towels?"

Mr. Dalton knelt on the floor and started to sop up the coffee.

"It's such an old rug," I commented. "Maybe this is a good thing. You could ask for a new rug. Your office needs some sprucing up anyway. Not that I don't like it, of course. I think you have great taste in pictures. I really like the stuff you have hanging on the walls. Where did you get that one of the duck playing golf?"

"Lindy." Mr. Dalton threw a wad of wet towels into his trash can. "Why don't you just sit down and I'll worry about cleaning this up a little later."

He sat behind his desk. The whole room smelled like carpet-flavored coffee. "It looks like the earthquake moved your folder, too," he said.

I slid down a little in my seat.

He flipped the folder open. His eyebrows shot up, but if he noticed the little changes to my permanent record, he didn't say so. "You've been here about five months now, is that right?"

"Uh-huh."

Mr. Dalton rustled through some more papers in the folder. He leaned his elbows on the desk and tapped his index fingers against his lips. "Lindy, I have a problem and I just can't figure it out. I need you to help me. OK?"

I nodded, just to be polite.

"Here it is. The papers in this folder tell me that you are a bright young lady. From kindergarten through sixth grade you attended Oxford Elementary in Philadelphia. You had fine grades not only in your academic subjects but in your conduct as well. Am I right so far?"

He wasn't out of the office long enough for me to

change any of that stuff. I just nodded again to keep him moving along. I was beginning to feel like one of those bobbing-head dolls.

"And now you've been at Mecong for five months, and not only are you in danger of failing math and science . . . "

"I'm more of a language person," I cut in.

Mr. Dalton held up his hand. "I also have three disciplinary complaints against you, and that's not even counting what happened on your first day."

"Three!?" I sat up in my chair.

"According to Mr. Pierce, you jabbed him in the back with a paper clip this morning in homeroom. Last month, there was that incident in the cafeteria with the lime Jell-O. And not one hour ago, Mrs. Tremont was sitting in that very chair talking to me about your behavior during a softball practice this weekend. What's going on with you, Lindy?"

"Nothing is going on with me!" I snapped. "I didn't do anything! I didn't. I can't help it if Melissa doesn't know how to catch a ball. If she can't pay attention when we're having a catch, maybe she should just switch to the glee club or something." I crossed my arms. I couldn't believe that Mrs. Tremont. She had better watch out next time she pitched to me because I know how to hit them straight at the mound. I'd show her.

Mr. Dalton looked at the papers in my folder again. He had short brown hair with little spots of gray all over, like dandruff. He wore his glasses down on the tip of his nose and kept glancing at me over the top of them. "Did you like moving from Philadelphia to Shelbourne?" he suddenly asked.

I had no idea why, but a huge lump formed right in the middle of my throat and I couldn't answer right away. "Oh, sure," I finally said. "It's great here." People from the suburbs think Philadelphia is the evil empire. If I said I liked it there, he would probably have sent me straight to the school psychologist.

"I see you spent a little bit of time in Leedstown also. What were you doing there?"

Now I was really getting mad. "Is this a trial or something?" I jumped out of the chair. Why should he care about Leedstown? It was none of his business. "I have to get to science class. We're having a big test on Wednesday."

I didn't wait for an answer. I ran for the hall. He'd probably send another letter home to my parents. That was OK. I knew how to intercept the mail.

10

◆ ◆ ◆

I GRABBED MY BOOKS from homeroom and headed down the empty staircase toward science. It can be spooky on those stairs when it's quiet and everyone else is in class. It's like being in a cinderblock cave, and it smells funny, like the inside of a musty old book. My footsteps echoed off the walls and my breathing sounded superloud, like Darth Vader's, that evil guy from *Star Wars*. I know it's really stupid, but I looked over my shoulder once to make sure he wasn't there. I finally decided that the weird noise had to be coming from me. As far as I could remember from the movie, Darth Vader didn't sniff. And he never cried, even when he was losing. That Mr. Dalton made me so mad. I wiped my eyes on the back of my sleeves. Crying is for babies and little kids like Randy. I don't cry.

I leaned against the rail. I didn't have a late pass and my science teacher, Mr. Franco, was annoyingly strict about that stuff. There was no way I was going to let him send me back to the office. I didn't need to go to science anyway. I never learned anything there. All my courses were stupid. They didn't teach any of the stuff a person really needed to know about life. I grabbed the top book from the pile in my arms, *Treasure Island*, and flung it down the steps. When it hit the floor, it made a little pop sound that echoed in the stairwell. Good-bye, useless pirates and stupid buried treasures. Next, I tried the fat science text. I threw it just right, like a lead Frisbee, and it smacked the floor with a satisfying boom. Good riddance to protons and neutrons and other useless invisible stuff. I tossed the binders next and then the notebooks. I sat on a step and watched some of the stray papers slide slowly down toward the landing.

I was wondering if anybody would miss me if I slipped out of the building for a few hours when I saw her face through the double doors down below. If I had known she was coming I would have waited to throw my books until she was in range.

The door squeaked open. "Lindy?" Mrs. Tremont came rushing up the steps toward me, her plastic ID badge flapping against her chest. "Are you OK? What happened?"

I let myself cry. It's OK to do it when you're just pretending and need the sympathy. "I tripped," I blubbered. "I think I twisted my ankle." I felt so sorry for myself I could almost feel the pain shooting through my bone.

"Let me get the nurse. Don't move."

I grabbed the handrail and pretended to struggle to my feet. "No, no," I insisted, quickly wiping my eyes. "It's OK. I'll be all right!" Nurse Baumgartner is one scary human being, and I would rather bleed to death on the front steps of the school with vultures picking at my eyes than go to her office. Besides, it would take her only half a second to know that I was faking.

"See?" I said. "I can walk on it."

Mrs. Tremont looked unconvinced. She bent down and felt my ankle, carefully flexing it one way and then another. "Does that hurt?" she asked. Her glasses had slipped all the way down to the edge of her nose, and she was peering at my ankle so closely that her frizzy hair was tickling my skin. When I thought about her ratting me out to Mr. Dalton, I felt like kicking her down the steps. The only thing that stopped me was that I didn't want to get suspended during softball season.

"No, it's fine. Really." I walked down the steps with just the slightest limp. "See?"

Mrs. Tremont followed me down. She picked up all my books and papers. She didn't even comment on the math quiz with the big red F on the top. She just tucked it into my folder with all the other junk. "I think we should get you checked out just to be on the safe side."

"No, Mrs. Tremont," I begged. "I'm fine. Please don't make me go."

Mrs. Tremont stared at me. Her arms were wrapped around my books, and her fingers tapped against my science text. "You don't like Tums?" she finally asked.

I didn't want to, but I had to smile. Mrs. Tremont actually had a sense of humor. "I hate them!" I complained. "Everybody does. But how did you know about the Tums?"

Nurse Baumgartner is an ancient, bony woman with a heart made out of pure steel. As soon as you open the door to her office, her beady eyes fix on you with loathing and suspicion. If you get sick at Mecong, you have to make sure that you catch some of your vomit on your clothes. It's the only proof she accepts. If you don't have any, she gives you two Tums and sends you back to class. Now I was wondering if maybe she treated the teachers the same way.

"Consider yourself lucky," Mrs. Tremont explained. "When I went to this school, Mrs. Baumgartner doled out some chalky liquid. Believe me, Tums taste a whole lot better."

"You were a student here?" I blurted. "I didn't know the school was that old!" I knew that didn't come out right, but I was truly surprised. My school in Philadelphia was so old that I think Betsy Ross might have gone there. Mecong looked really modern in comparison. The toilets all flushed, and none of the ceilings leaked during rainstorms. The library here had about a million more books, and as far as I could tell, they were so new that none of them predicted that man would land on the moon someday soon.

Mrs. Tremont just stared at me.

I tried to recover. "What I meant was . . . I'm new here and all . . . and I just thought that, you know, the school was really new. It looks new. Don't you think it looks new?"

Mrs. Tremont just shook her head at me. "Come on, you. Out into the hall. I want to see you walk. Then I'll decide whether you can skip the Tums."

We walked the length of three classrooms before she was satisfied. "I swear it doesn't hurt," I pleaded.

Mrs. Tremont crossed her arms and looked me up and down. "I know you hide pain well, Lindy. Are you sure you are telling me the truth? It's not worth walking on it if it hurts. You'll just injure it more."

For the first time since I've known her, I was telling the truth. "Cross my heart and hope to die."

"All right," she sighed, "but take it easy." She turned to go.

"Mrs. Tremont!" I whispered after her. "Do you think that you could let me have a late pass? I had one, of course. I really did. It's just that when all my stuff fell down the steps, it must have gotten lost."

Even though I could tell she didn't believe my excuse, Mrs. Tremont scribbled out the pass for me. She slapped it into my open hand. "Where's your class?" she asked.

I pointed across the hall.

"Then get in it."

I started to leave.

"Oh, Lindy, wait," she called.

I turned. "Yes?"

"I want you to have your parents give me a call. I mean it."

"Oh. OK. But you should know we're having some trouble with our phone."

She grimaced, but one side of her mouth curled up just a little bit, and I think maybe she was trying hard not to smile. "So I've noticed," she said.

Mrs. Tremont knows I'm lying, but she still can't figure out how to beat me. She stood with folded arms and watched until I had gone into my science classroom.

I handed the late slip to Mr. Franco and slid into my seat. I didn't pay attention to the science lecture, but I did learn two things today: Mrs. Tremont has a sense of humor, and she actually used to be a kid.

11

◆ ◆ ◆

"But I have a game!" I hissed at Freddy, a little too loudly. "I can't watch him and play at the same time!"

My teammates were cocking their heads in our direction, trying to soak up every word. I had been warming up and I had a bat in my hand. It is just lucky for Freddy that he was on the other side of the fence. Randy was sitting in the dirt pile, crying again.

"You don't have to watch him every second. It's not as if he's going to run away or anything," Freddy argued. "Just let him hang out here and take him home after the game."

"Why can't he stay with you?"

"I got stuff I gotta do."

I slammed the bat into the fence and Freddy jumped back. I knew what stuff he had to do. I could see Melanie, his girlfriend, waiting for him off the first base line.

"Isn't Dad home?" I was grasping for straws.

"No. He's wandering around somewhere. Come on, Lindy. What's the big deal?"

Randy's shoulders were shaking and the dirt pile would soon turn into mud from the rivers flowing out of his eyes. The whole team was watching us now. They weren't even pretending to warm up. I had to get Freddy out of here before he gave away all our family secrets.

"Just go," I said through clenched teeth. I dropped my bat and walked around the fence.

"C'mon, Randy." I picked him up and he rested his head on my shoulder. He stuck his dirty thumb in his mouth. I carried him over to an empty part of the bleachers, away from all the stares of my nosy teammates.

"Sorry, Lindy," he sniffed. His arms were around my neck, and I could feel the little heaves in his chest that he always gets when he cries too much.

"Don't you be sorry. I'm glad you're here, Randy," I said, smoothing out his tangled hair. "You're like our team mascot. I know we're going to do better in our game today because you're here."

He lifted his head from my shoulder. "Really?" Sometimes it's a good thing that he's so gullible.

"Really," I said. "I was just mad at Freddy because he never does anything he's supposed to do." That Freddy cares only about himself. If he isn't sleeping, he's partying or hanging out with his friends. Nothing ever seems to bother him. He even told his friends about Rebecca and what happened. When they came to our house for the first time, some of them said, "Sorry about your little daughter, Mrs. Perkins." Then they sat on the couch and laughed and ate potato chips. I bet he even told them that we lived in the homeless shelter. He makes me so mad.

"Freddy's going to the movies." Randy wiped his eyes on his sleeves. "But it's a big-person movie and I can't go."

I used the edge of my uniform to clean the dirt streaks from Randy's face. "That's OK," I said, "because this game is going to be way more exciting than any old movie."

The bus had pulled up in the parking lot while I was talking to Randy, and the Pickertown Pirates were heading toward the field. Mrs. Tremont shook hands with their coach, then walked straight over to me.

She laid her hand on Randy's head. "Why doesn't Randy sit on the bench with us?"

Randy buried his face in my shirt.

"No, thanks, Mrs. Tremont," I answered. "I think that Randy likes it better in the dirt pile. That way he can play and he doesn't have to have somebody touching his head every two minutes and treating him like some kind of pet."

Mrs. Tremont slowly pulled her hand off Randy's curls. Without saying another word she turned and walked away.

I guess I ticked her off again. Too bad for her. I stood up and Randy tumbled from my lap. He followed me over to the dirt pile, but he wouldn't stay. Because it was game day, there were other little kids there. Two boys were wrestling at the top, trying to push each other off. A little girl was playing with what must have been either Ditchdigger Barbie or Coal Miner Barbie. The poor doll was covered in grime, and the girl was trying to shove her into a hole she had carved in the dirt. Randy took one look and clung to my shorts.

"Don't be such a baby!" I pried his fingers off my uniform. I held him by the shoulders. "You play with these kids," I said. "You have fun."

"Lindy!" Randy whispered and pulled on my shirt.

"What?"

"That's Becca's doll," he whined, pointing to a toddler dragging a bald-headed baby doll behind her.

"It is not," I said. "It just looks the same. Now knock it off." Besides Rebecca leaving us and Randy getting taken away for a few days by the social-service people, I think the next-hardest thing for him to handle was the fact that after we moved, all of Rebecca's things disappeared. I'm pretty sure my mother gave them all away. Everywhere he goes, every time he sees a pull-toy dog or a hug-me wiggle worm in some other kid's hand, he thinks the kid has Rebecca's toy. I know I should probably be patient and understanding, but it is getting on my nerves.

"But it's . . . " He tried to argue. He wanted it back. He wants everything back.

"It's not hers!" I shouted. I couldn't help myself. I slapped his hand off my uniform.

I stalked around the fence to the bench. Randy

followed me. "No way, mister," I said. I grabbed the back of his shirt and shoved him back behind the fence. "Only the players can come in here," I lied. "You go play with those kids."

"Lindy!" Gabby cried. "Let him come in here with us! He's sooo cute. We'll take care of him."

Mae and Brigid started making cooing noises and the whole team was nodding its big collective, empty, stupid head.

"No. N-O," I said. "He stays out. O-U-T. Got it? You leave him alone." They'd ask him too many prying questions. And I could watch him just fine if he stayed in the dirt pile. I grabbed my glove and pushed through my teammates. I stalked out to first base. I stood there alone. I had forgotten to bring a ball.

While I waited for everyone to take the field, I scanned the stands. As usual, Kelly's mother was there with the little Kellys. I call her brothers and sister that because they all look exactly alike — red hair, freckles, and smiling skinny faces. The whole darned happy family comes to every game. I don't even know why they come. Kelly hardly ever gets to play. They just sit there looking cheerful and clapping for everything. They waved at me.

"Is that your mom?"

I whirled around. Eric was standing beside the bag, his hands in his pockets.

"Oh . . . um, no. My mom has a real important job, and she has to work a lot. She really hates it that she can't be here. She wanted to hire some guy to come and videotape all my games so she could watch them late at night when she got home from work, but I said, like, no way. That would be too incredibly embarrassing. My grandmother used to come to all my games, though. But she's been sick and so she can't make it today. We're just waiting for some test results to see if she's going to be able to come next week." I had to bite on my lower lip to shut myself up. I swear my mouth is like the Pennypack Creek after a downpour. It just keeps gushing and gushing, stirring up all kinds of useless trash.

Eric was staring at me. There was an awkward silence that lasted long enough for me to wish about one million times that I had brought a ball out with me. At least I'd have something to do besides stare at my shoes.

Eric finally came up with something. "How about your dad? Is he here?"

Suddenly, I liked the awkward silence better. "Oh. My dad? No, he's . . . he's working on some real important stuff or he'd be here."

"Yeah, my dad works a lot, too. It really stinks. He's an investment banker."

"That's cool. My dad, he um . . . he designs stuff . . . for his company." I said it real fast and mumbly. At least it was partially true. He designs all kinds of strange stuff in the backyard.

"What kind of stuff does he . . . "

"What do you think of our new uniforms?" I cut in. I held my arms out and modeled like those ladies on the game shows who stand beside grand-prize refrigerators and try to make them look exciting.

Eric gave me an approving glance. "They're cool."

"Yeah. I like the lightning bolt best. It's pretty sharp." Our uniforms are black with two gold stripes down the sides. The lightning bolt starts up at the right shoulder and cuts across the whole front of the shirt. I know this sounds pretty weird, but when I put my uniform on, I kind of feel like Clark Kent ducking into the phone booth and coming out like Superman. Even Melissa can't make fun of me in this uniform. I feel all-powerful. The great Lindy Perkins, bound for fame. No one would ever guess that I am really a strange kid who lives next to a hubcap tree, with a crazy father, a trembly little brother, and a big, ugly secret. It almost makes me forget.

I felt a dull thud in the middle of my back. A ball dropped at my feet.

"Gee, I'm soooo sorry." Melissa smirked at me. "The ball must have slipped."

"No problem," I called out to right field. "These things happen. Lucky for me you have such a weak arm."

With enormous relief, I saw my teammates taking the field. I tossed the ball to second. "I better warm up some," I said to Eric.

"Sure. You're still coming to the party, right?"

I kicked the toe of my spikes against the bag. "Yeah. I guess so," I answered.

"Have a good game."

Eric walked off. I tried to act like I wasn't watching. He climbed up into the stands with some of his friends.

I WAS GUARDING FIRST. There was a runner on the bag. I don't pay much attention to their faces when I'm playing, just their feet and legs, the way they lean. I know their position and how they bat. I know their speed. This girl was the Pirate's right fielder, lean and muscled. She could fly. I never looked at her face until she spoke to me.

"Hey, aren't you Lindy, the shelter kid? What are you doing in Shelbourne?"

My eyes jumped to her face. It was Morgan Whistler, from Leedstown, one of the biggest jerks at Franklin Elementary. She used to torture Ramón, a pint-sized second-grader who lived at the shelter, too, and played with Randy sometimes. Ramón had a pretty bad lisp, and a lot of kids made fun of him. But Morgan was the worst, and she was old enough to know better. Morgan and I had had a bunch of fights.

"I'm playing softball, you moron." I punched my fist into my glove and held it out toward Dana, our pitcher, pretending I was waiting for the pick-off throw. Morgan moved back toward the bag, a slight smile on her face.

"What are you, some kind of charity case here?"

Dana wound up and the batter held her bat way above her head. Morgan took a small lead. The ball thumped into the catcher's mitt. Strike one.

Morgan stepped back to the bag.

"You must be the charity case," I snarled. "I can't believe they put you on this team. Who'd you pay off?"

Morgan smirked. "We know you didn't pay anybody off, shelter kid, since you've got nothing. Slept under any good bridges lately?"

Dana's next pitch was slightly outside, and the batter knocked it foul down the first base line. I made a run for it, but it was too far out. I picked the ball out of the grass and fired it back to Dana. Dust flew out of her glove as the ball smacked into it. It was the top of the fourth of a six-inning game; the Pirates were up on us, three to two. Morgan was their only base runner with two outs.

"Are you still as slow as ever?" I asked Morgan, keeping an eye on Dana's windup.

"Slow?" Morgan snorted. "I could beat you any day, shelter kid."

"You're looking pretty slow to me. Have you put on some weight?"

Dana threw a ball high and outside. The count was one and two.

"I bet you can't steal," I taunted. "I bet you're too slow to make it to second. How many doughnuts did you have before the game?"

"Second is a piece of cake, shelter kid." Morgan sure liked that shelter word. "I can take it anytime I want."

Dana was in the middle of her delivery. It was low, ball two.

"Chicken." I said it low, under my breath, but loud enough for Morgan to hear. I didn't look at her, but I saw the muscles in her legs tense.

Dana needed only one more out. She had two strikes on the batter. She wasn't paying any attention to the runner on first. She hadn't even thrown one my way to keep the runner close. But she would real soon.

"Come on, Dana, Dana. Let's go, Dana, Dana. You can do it, Dana, Dana," I chanted. I never do any of those useless cheers just for the heck of it. This was my code way of telling Dana that the runner on first was going to make a run for it. I only chant when I'm about 90 percent sure. I thought up this system all by myself. We used it on my neighborhood team in Philadelphia and it worked pretty well. I knew I had suckered Morgan into making a run for it, and she was too stupid to know that I was letting Dana and Jo, our catcher, know about it.

Dana never even looked at first. She went into her windup. Just as she released, Jo jumped up from behind the plate and caught the pitchout. She rifled the ball to Meg at second. Morgan was caught. She was halfway between first and second, undecided. Meg had a big smile on her face. Morgan whirled and tried to make it back to first. Meg whipped the ball to me. Morgan tried a head-first slide. I had it covered. I slapped her good and hard with my glove before her outstretched hands could touch the bag.

"Out!" the umpire called.

Morgan groaned and rolled over in the dirt. I stepped over her as I headed for the bench. "Nice try," I sneered. "Better skip those doughnuts before the next game."

Dana and Jo high-fived me. I took a swig out of my water bottle. It sure was hot out here. Randy might need a drink, too. I took a quick look around, but he wasn't beside the fence or in the dirt pile.

"Randy!" I jumped off the bench.

"He's in the bleachers," Kelly said. "Look. Isn't it cute?"

Randy was sucking on a lollipop, Kelly's redheaded brothers giggling away just to his left. On his right was Eric! And Randy was blabbing to him. What could he possibly be talking about? Randy never talks to strangers. Why couldn't he just play in the dirt pile like a normal kid? Who knows what he could be saying to Eric. I had enough to worry about with big-mouth Morgan the Moron here. What if she told my teammates where I came from?

We lived at the homeless shelter for only about four months, but it felt like ten years. My mom said I shouldn't feel bad about it. She said that everybody needs help sometimes. But I never knew anybody who needed it that bad.

We slept in a room with cots all lined up in rows, real close. It was so crowded. I just couldn't sleep with all those people coughing and snoring and whistling through their noses all night. I just lay there in the dark and thought about what happened, so mad that I couldn't change it. And lots of times I made up my mind to tell Dad the truth, that it was my fault. But I never did it. I chickened out every time.

After it happened, Dad turned into a complete zombie. He just stood there and stared into space. The police asked lots of questions. Dad just kept saying over and over that it was all his fault, that he did it — nothing else. I sat in a chair. The words were in my throat to tell them what really happened. But I left them there. I didn't confess. They scared me. They had deep voices and thick belts with guns and sticks hanging from them. When they asked me my name, I said it real low into my lap because I didn't like them looking at me.

I was just eleven then. I didn't want them to arrest me. I thought that maybe they might if they knew. There was a kid in my school once named Jerry who pushed another kid out a window. He got sent away someplace and he never came back. I didn't want to get sent away. I figured I could tell the truth later, after they were gone.

I didn't know they were going to take Dad away with them. Then the social-service people took Randy and me away from our house. By the time Mom got us all back together again, except for Rebecca, it was too late. It was just too late to tell.

Dad stopped going to work. He spent all his time in the garage just banging on stuff. Mom didn't have a job. She always stayed home and took care of us kids. Nobody paid her for that. So we ran out of money real fast. When we had nothing left to pay our rent, we had to leave. Mrs. O'Malley, my friend Pauline's mom, offered to let me live with her and Pauline until my parents got things straightened out. But my mom said no. She said that we were a family and families have to stick together no matter what. So that's how we all ended up in the homeless shelter. Somebody helped my mom get the job at the hospital, and my aunt Cass in California sent us some money to tide us over. The house on the highway was the only thing near the hospital that we could afford to rent — and no wonder. I doubt that there is anyone else in all of Shelbourne who would be caught dead living in that house.

There've been lots of times since then when I wanted real bad to tell Dad that it wasn't his fault. Maybe he'd come back to us and be like he was before. But I just can't seem to do it. I know now I'm not going to go to jail or anything. But I'm still afraid. I'm afraid of how Mom might look at me. I'm afraid of what Dad will think of me for keeping quiet all this time. I wish I could tell them. It hangs on me so heavy, sometimes I feel like I just can't breathe.

I looked over at the bleachers and saw Randy laughing with Eric. I smiled a little bit. I felt bad, but I still had to go yank Randy out of there. It was too dangerous. You just never knew what he might say.

"Lindy! Where do you think you are going?" Mrs. Tremont was glaring at me, tapping a pencil on her clipboard.

"I'm just checking on Randy," I explained.

"You are not. He is fine. He's sitting in the bleachers with Kelly's family, and you are up right after Gabby. Get your helmet on and warm up."

I glanced at my brother again. He was holding his lollipop out toward Eric and Eric was smiling.

"RANDY!" I screamed. "DON'T YOU BE BOTHERING HIM!" It was the best I could do under the circumstances.

I pulled the helmet on my head and grabbed my bat. I watched Gabby at the plate. She had worked the count to three and two. The Pirates' pitcher was throwing hard. Gabby fouled one off over the backstop. The dirt-pile kids chased it down. The next pitch came in at about belt level, just like Gabby likes them. There was a loud crack and the ball sailed over the first baseman's head. Gabby ran like a truck, but she still made it to second. A lead-off runner with no outs.

I took a few practice swings. My teammates began to cheer me on. I already had one home run this game, but I wanted another one. I said a little silent prayer. I wanted to hit it right over Morgan's head. If possible, I wouldn't mind it going through her mouth on its way over the fence. I don't know if God would appreciate that last request, though. So I just prayed for the home run.

I stood over the plate. I swear, it's my favorite place on earth. I wish I could live here and bat all day long. I scraped my spikes through the dirt and tapped the bat on the edge of the plate three times for good luck. I was ready.

The pitcher turned on the mound and looked at Morgan in right. She gave her a thumbs-up. Morgan began a chant. "Give me an S!"

Some of her teammates answered, "S!"

"Give me an H!"

"H!" They screamed.

The pitcher whipped the ball over the plate.

"Strike one," called the umpire.

"I wasn't ready!" I protested.

"You were in the box, hon," the umpire said. "The strike counts. It's O and one."

I knew she was right, but I was still mad. I was more determined than ever to put the ball in Morgan's mouth. I adjusted my stance.

"Give me an E!"

"E!" Most of the Pirates were chiming in now.

"Give me an L!"

"L!"

The next pitch was a ball, low and inside. It almost got my ankle. I hopped out of the way just in time.

"Give me a T!"

"T!"

I could see my teammates on the bench looking at each other in bewilderment. This wasn't a chant that any of them had ever heard before. But I did. I heard it in many different forms when I was at Franklin Elementary. I knew what the last few letters would be. I had to hit the next pitch and shut them up. The ball was way high, but I swung anyway. I missed everything. Strike two.

"Give me an E!"

"E!"

"Give me an R!"

"R!"

"Just pitch the stupid ball," I screamed at the pitcher. "You wanna sing, or do you wanna play softball?"

"What's it spell?" Morgan was in a hurry, too.

"Shelter kid!" They yelled.

"Morgan, you stupid moron! You can't even spell!" She had forgotten the K-I-D. She didn't need it, though. Her teammates knew what was coming. I shot a quick glance over to my bench. Most of the kids were standing, their fingers curled through the chain link fence. Were they looking at me funny?

At the last second I realized that the next pitch was coming in. I swung, knowing that I was missing by a mile. I let go of the bat, hoping it would make it to right field. But it didn't get past second. The crowd let out a big "ooooh" as the bat clunked to the ground. I stalked to the bench and sat, my head in my hands.

"So, Lindy." Melissa put one foot up on the bench and leaned in toward me. "What was that all about?"

"I have no idea."

"Really?" She was chewing gum and she cracked it a few times until she had everyone's attention. "What does shelter kid mean?"

I jumped off the bench. "I told you. I have no idea! How am I supposed to know?"

"Well," Melissa drawled, "it just seems weird. That girl in right field seems to know you."

"I never saw her before."

"Then how come you know her name? You called her Morgan."

I sucked in my breath, momentarily frozen. "She told me her name, OK? She told me last inning when she was on first."

"Oh, right," Melissa droned. She rolled her eyes for the benefit of the team. "Like a base runner is going to formally introduce herself to you. I tell you what I think. I think . . . "

"Melissa!" Mrs. Tremont called out sharply.

"Yeah?"

"How many hits have you had this game?"

"Uh, none?"

"Right. You're up next, and we still have Gabby stranded on second. Maybe you should be warming up your swing instead of flapping your lips. Get out there."

Melissa hurried away, and I sat at the edge of the bench, my back to everyone.

Kelly slid up next to me. "Don't listen to Melissa," she said. "She's just jealous of you."

"Thanks, Kel," I mumbled. It was a nice thing to say, even if it was laughably untrue. Sure, I was the better softball player. But Melissa was prettier, richer, much more popular, and she probably never lost her little sister or sent her family to the homeless shelter.

We lost the game, but that wasn't the worst of it.

AFTER THE FINAL OUT we always have to get in a straight line and slap hands with the other team. I don't mind it so much when we win. But when we lose, it can be really annoying.

I was last in our line. "Good game," we all mumbled to each other, shuffling our feet through the dirt.

I had my eyes on the ground, but I could hear Morgan coming. "Good game, fatso," she said to Gabby, who was two in front of me. "Nice strike out, carrot head," she scoffed at Kelly.

I was ready when she reached me. "You smell, shelter kid. You stink as much as ever." Morgan's hand was raised, just like everyone else's, but I managed to miss it. I gave her a good one-handed shove in the shoulder and she stumbled back a few feet. She jumped forward and pushed me in the same way. I felt my hands clench into fists and I took a swing at her ugly face. I would have hit her, too, except that Mrs. Tremont grabbed the back of my shirt and jerked me out of line.

"On the bench. Now." She pointed her long bony arm, as if I didn't know where the bench was anyway.

I would have argued with her, but I didn't feel like slapping hands with the rest of the Pirates. So I went to the bench.

Mrs. Tremont gathered the team and gave us all the usual pep talk. We played a good game, we made a few mistakes, we need to work on some things in practice. It's always the same, win or lose. I think she should tape-record it. Or maybe she could write a book and give us all a copy — *Mrs. Tremont's Terrifically Boring and Bogus Speeches*. When we're done playing, she could just tell us to turn to page 97 for the postgame speech. When anybody's late for practice, she could just direct her to the punctuality speech on page 12. Then there would be the "I won't accept that kind of language around here speech" and the "I want to see some more effort out of you" speech. Just think of all the time a book like that could save.

I was so busy thinking of this great book that I didn't notice the talking was over and kids were starting to leave. I got up to go, but Mrs. Tremont leaned on my shoulder and pushed me right back down.

"You're staying," she said. "I need to have a talk with you."

I sighed. This speech book could end up as fat as the Bible.

"Lindy! Lindy!" Randy came running my way. It was the first time in ages that he had raised his voice above the usual whimper. He was actually shouting. "Look what Eric gave me!"

I pulled Randy onto my lap and looked around for Eric. He was headed toward the parking lot, but he turned and gave us a wave.

"This is really cool." I stroked the shiny red Matchbox car and wondered. How did Eric know that Randy would be at the game? He must have brought it just in case.

"Look," Randy said, grasping the car in his grubby little fingers. "The door even opens and closes. But there's no driver inside."

"So what did you and Eric talk about?"

Randy flipped the miniature trunk open and held it in front of my face. He had put a teeny, tiny pebble inside. His face beamed. "Just stuff," he finally answered.

"What kind of stuff?"

"I don't know. He just asked me questions and stuff."

"About what?" I could feel my heart start to pound faster.

Mrs. Tremont had finished cleaning up the equipment, and she lifted Randy right off my lap. "Why don't you go and try out your new car on the other bench, Randy? I need to talk to Lindy for a minute."

"OK." Randy ran off making airplane noises, his new car zooming through the air.

I decided to distract her, to get her thinking about the game instead of me shoving that good-for-nothing

Morgan. "I'm sorry for that last at bat, Mrs. Tremont. I know I messed it up. I know we could have won that game. It's because . . . "

Mrs. Tremont held up her hand. "I am not concerned about whether we won or lost, Lindy."

I dropped my mouth open and pretended to be shocked. I couldn't let her sidetrack my plan. "Well, Mrs. Tremont, I don't want to be disrespectful here, but what's the point of you being a coach, because aren't we supposed to try to win games? I mean, I thought that was, like, the goal of playing the game." I shook my head in disgust. I tried to get up. Mrs. Tremont towers over me even when I'm standing on my tiptoes. Sitting here made me feel smaller than ever, and I was getting tired of staring straight at her knobby knees. I made it halfway before she pushed me right back down on the bench. I thought that teachers weren't allowed to touch students. That was twice now. I could probably sue her for that.

"We're not done talking here, Lindy." She let out one of her big sighs and sat down beside me. "You may not get to play many more games on this team. Are you aware of that?"

"What?!" This time she couldn't stop me from jumping up. "Just because I pushed that girl? She's such a jerk. You would've pushed her, too. You didn't hear the stuff she was saying to everybody. All I did was . . . "

"Lindy," Mrs. Tremont grabbed my arm. "Sit down. That is only part of your problem."

That was three times she touched me. I wasn't going to forget it, either.

"You are not permitted to play or practice with any school team if you have a failing grade on your report card. Mr. Dalton tells me that you are close to failing both math and science. Do you need help?"

I let my head fall into my hands. "No."

"Mr. Dalton says that you have plenty of ability. You're just not putting out the effort, Lindy. What's the problem?"

I jumped off the bench again. "There is no problem! Mr. Dalton doesn't know anything, and neither do you!" I tried to leave, but Mrs. Tremont was quicker. She stood in front of the gate and blocked my exit.

"Why don't you fill me in, then?" she said.

"I need to go home now."

"I'm trying to help you here, Lindy."

"I need to go home now," I said through clenched teeth. "I don't need any help."

Mrs. Tremont wouldn't budge out of my way. "We also need to discuss your outbursts, Lindy. You cannot shove a player from another team, no matter how obnoxious she is. And you certainly cannot hit a player on your own team with a ball. Why don't you tell me what is going on with you?"

"I did not hit Melissa with the ball!" I shouted. "It's not my fault that she can't catch!" I had enough of this.

"Lindy, you . . . "

I climbed the fence and jumped to freedom. Randy was running his car along a bench. I wished I had kept him next to me. "C'mon, Randy," I called, clapping my hands together. "Let's go. We gotta get home. Right now!"

But Mrs. Tremont intercepted my brother and took his hand in hers.

"Randy, you come here!" I ordered.

Randy looked up at Mrs. Tremont. She didn't let go of his hand. "I'm giving you and your brother a ride home today."

"We don't need a ride. We can walk."

Mrs. Tremont just turned and strode toward her dumpy car, dragging my little brother behind her.

"It's healthier to walk!" I screamed. "It's not even very far!" I threw my glove as far as I could toward the woods.

Randy looked at me over his shoulder. He wasn't even crying. Just when I need him to bawl his eyes out, he gets all calm on me. Mrs. Tremont put Randy in the backseat and buckled him in. I stood in the field, staring at the car. The sky was getting dark, and a slow rumble of thunder slid across the fields and disappeared behind the school.

I had no choice. I had to go with Randy. Without me to keep him in line, he would tell Mrs. Tremont anything she wanted to know. And he would lead her right to our house and ruin everything. I grabbed my glove and headed for the car. I prayed that a bolt of lightning would puncture holes in Mrs. Tremont's tires.

At least she didn't try to force me into the front seat this time. I moved aside an empty coffee cup and some fast-food wrappers and slid into the back. There was barely room for my feet. Old mail and a ratty blanket and pillow littered the floor. Randy ran his car up the side of the door.

"Do you live in your car?" I blurted.

She sighed and turned on the motor. "Sometimes it feels as if I do."

"Do you know you got a pillow back here?"

"I'm aware of what is in my car, Lindy."

"Are you married?" I wasn't going to give her a chance.

"Yes."

"What does your husband do? Is he a teacher?"

The car stalled at a stop sign and Mrs. Tremont sat still for a moment, leaning on the steering wheel. I thought for a minute that she was going to fall asleep right there, and Randy and I could make our escape. But the car suddenly jerked into gear.

She didn't answer the husband question. "You got any kids?" I pressed.

If she had any kids, I bet she lost them lots of times under piles of clothes and old papers. I drummed my fingers on an old shoebox on the backseat. Someone had written Medical Records on it, but you had to look close to see it. It was all faded. Maybe Mrs. Tremont wasn't healthy. That would explain why she was cranky all the time.

Mrs. Tremont ignored me and drove straight to River Meadows. But she didn't stop at the McCallisters' house.

"You passed it!" I called. "Stop the car!"

"I did not pass it." Mrs. Tremont was driving real slow now, peering at the numbers on the mailboxes. "You do not live at number 34, Lindy. You're at 46."

I swallowed hard. "I'm twelve years old, you know. I should know where I live! Stop the car! Stop it!" I ripped my seat belt off.

Mrs. Tremont did stop the car, right in front of our gravel driveway. She turned in her seat and stared at me. "I'd like to come in and talk to one of your parents for a few minutes."

I felt a giant ball of fire explode in my stomach. "You can't! They're not home. They're at work. They don't want to talk to you anyway."

I bolted out of the car, pulling Randy behind me. We raced up the driveway. Mom really was at work, but I was worried about Dad. When we made it to the porch, I took a quick look over my shoulder. Mrs. Tremont had started to follow me. She was standing just inside the bushes. I couldn't hide the hubcap tree or the mannequin-head pole or any of the strange trash sculptures, but at least Dad wasn't there. I could see her eyes squinting, taking in everything in our yard. A shiver went through me.

"Leave us alone!" I shouted at her. My voice came out all thick and funny. "Our dog bites strangers!" I stomped inside with Randy and slammed and locked the door.

"Lindy!" Randy pulled on my shirt. "Lindy! We don't have a dog."

I shoved him out of the way and peeked at Mrs. Tremont through the window. Thunder rolled overhead, and this time the rain came with it. But Mrs. Tremont still stood in the yard. It was weird, but she sort of fit in there, all gawky and strange — her short hair plastered to her head, her glasses sticking out on the end of her big nose. She came up onto the porch and pushed the doorbell button about five times. Of course, our doorbell doesn't work, just like everything else in this stupid house. She never tried knocking. Maybe she was afraid of what my parents would look like, living in a house like this. She probably thought my dad had no teeth and answered the door with a big, long shotgun under his arm. Maybe she thought that a hard knock would cause the whole place to fall down. When she finally turned and left, she did it slowly, so that it looked like she was melting away in the rain. I think I won again.

Dad was sitting on the couch, watching the Phillies game, and he turned his head when we came in and smiled at us. Randy had flopped on the floor and was working on one of his puzzles. My hands were still shaking and I stuck them into my pockets. I sank into the couch next to Dad and rested my head on his shoulder. He ran his hand through my hair, like in the old days, and I started dreaming of fairy tales. I wished that life could turn out like fairy tales. Sleeping Beauties wake up, and poisoned Snow Whites get healthy again. I could mix up a magic potion and give it to Dad to drink. There would be a poof, his body would tremble slightly, and then he would be back to his old self.

Leaning against him, I could hear his heart beating. "You know what I think, Dad?"

"What?" He was still stroking my hair.

"I think fairy tales are wrong."

"Wrong?"

"Yeah. 'Cause life's not like a fairy tale. You don't always get happy endings."

Dad's hand froze. I felt the tips of his fingers tense against my scalp. I knew I should have kept my thoughts to myself.

"Never mind. That was stupid," I quickly added. "Just pretend I didn't say a word."

Dad put his arm around my shoulder and squeezed me real tight. He kissed the top of my head. "There's some work I gotta do," he said, standing.

I heard the screen door click shut. I threw myself back on the evil couch and buried my face in the cushions. I prayed that I would get sucked in and disappear from the face of the earth. And then it occurred to me: I do have the magic words that can break Dad out of his spell. I just have to use them. I have to tell him the truth.

I must have fallen asleep, because when the front door slammed, I didn't even know where I was.

Freddy stood over me. "Pizza," he said, his shaggy hair hanging over his eyes. "And I got you a present for watching Randy today."

Now I knew that I must be asleep. This had to be a dream. I tried to get up, but the couch had sucked in my whole right arm and a good part of my leg, too. Freddy grabbed my left hand and pulled me out.

"It's on the table," he said.

14

◆ ◆ ◆

MOM TUCKED MY HAIR behind my ears and smiled. "You look sweet."

"Mom! Give me a break!" I shook my head and jerked away from her. I did not look sweet. I didn't feel sweet, either. I think the last time that I was sweet I was three years old. I've been kind of mangy ever since then.

Randy is sweet. So is Rebecca. Our old next-door neighbor, Mrs. Paulson, always used to say, "That Rebecca is so sweet I could just eat her up." What a stupid saying. Mrs. Paulson reminded me of the witch from "Hansel and Gretel," dreaming of fattening up Rebecca for a tasty dinner. Whenever Dad told us that story, I pictured the house next door made out of candy and Rebecca squeezed into a little cage in the middle of the dining-room table. When I ran errands for Mrs. Paulson, I made sure not to go inside with my deliveries.

"I wish I had something new to wear," I complained, smoothing out my shirt.

"Sweetheart, you look beautiful. Anyway, it doesn't matter what you wear. People like you for who you are, not for the kind of clothes you wear." My mother is clueless.

I had on a pair of jeans, some old scuffed-up shoes, and a striped green shirt that used to belong to somebody named Francine. I made Mom cut her name out of the shirt before I agreed to put it on. What kind of a dork puts her name in her shirt anyway? This was even more evidence that my outfit was dorky. Maybe Francine was a twin, Mom suggested, and didn't want her clothes confused with her sister's. I was doomed.

I was mad at myself for ever agreeing to go to Eric's party in the first place. I tried to fake a last-minute illness, but Kelly said that she was coming to pick me up no matter what. She didn't swallow the gas leak story either, and I finally had to give her the McCallisters' address. And now my mom was fussing over me as if I was headed out to the prom.

"Do you want to put on a little of my makeup?" Mom followed me out onto the porch.

"No way!" I had experimented with her makeup before. I ended up looking like Bozo the Clown. "It's just a party, Mom."

"I know, I know," she sighed. "But it's your first girl-boy party. You're growing up."

I wish I wasn't growing up. I wish I was growing down. I wouldn't mind being four again, when the worst thing you had to worry about was some kid hogging all the blocks during playtime in your preschool. The truth about twelve is that it's a pretty awful age to be. I know I'm supposed to want to slather on the makeup and get my ears pierced in several different places and wear skintight clothes. But I don't. Sometimes I wonder if there is something seriously wrong with me. Kelly reads a lot of girl magazines, and she's always trying to get me to take the quizzes that are supposed to reveal things like "Is it a crush, or is it love?" and "Your perfect date." I won't ever answer the questions, though. I'm afraid that my survey will reveal that I'm a loser or that my perfect date would be with a chimpanzee.

My mom started playing with my hair again. I had to get out of here. Besides, I couldn't let Kelly get to the McCallisters' before I did. "I'm just going to wait for Kelly out by the street, Mom. See ya."

She put her arms around me and gave me a hug. It lasted a little too long and I finally had to wiggle free. "I gotta go, Mom."

"OK." She let her arms slip from my shoulders. "Have fun!" she called after me.

I took one look back when I got to the end of the driveway. Mom was in her chair, rocking away, her thin brown hair swaying back and forth against her face.

I waved, but she was staring past me, into the distance.

I sat on the curb in front of the McCallisters' and stared at the surprise Freddy had brought home for me the other night. It was a new CD that he said everybody wanted. I only wished he had had enough brains to have picked up some wrapping paper as well. I know it's bad to think this, but I wondered if Freddy stole it from the Eckles Drug Store. I couldn't imagine him spending his money on me. I rubbed the box on my pant leg. The least I could do was shine it up. Eric probably already had ten copies, though.

I stared at the picture of the rap group on the cover. I know I am not cool, but I hate coming across evidence of that fact every hour or two. I had no idea who these guys were. They looked like they shopped at the same thrift store as my mother, only they did a much-worse job. They had some painful-looking piercings and awful hairdos.

All of a sudden, I felt a hot breath down the back of my neck. At first I thought it was probably just my nerves from worrying about this stupid party. I'd been breaking out in sweats for days now every time I thought about it. But then I felt it again. I had a bad feeling. I slowly turned my head. My heart stopped and every part of my body started tingling. I was face-to-face with the Petra dogs! They were so close, I could smell their dog breath. I screamed and jumped ten feet into the road. A car screeched to a halt just inches in front of me, and I leaped up onto the hood. Those Petra dogs had sneaked up on me. If I had given them one more second, they would have sunk their teeth right into my neck. They were barking like crazy now, jumping up at me, their big paws clicking on the side of the car.

"Lindy!" Kelly jumped out of the car. "What are you doing?"

I was kind of glad that it was her and not some stranger in the car. But her question sure was stupid. "I'm saving my skin," I explained, panting as loud as those dogs. "What does it look like?"

Kelly's mother was staring at me through the windshield, and I was afraid that maybe she had gone into shock. She had this bug-eyed, open-mouth look frozen on her face, and her hands were gripping the steering wheel so hard that I could see the whites of her knuckles from out here on the hood.

Little Stephanie slid out of the car behind Kelly and started petting the dogs. They licked her face.

"Watch out!" I called to Kelly. "They're just tasting what flavor she is. They'll swallow her in one gulp."

I saw Mrs. Petra hurrying up the street. I tried to look natural up there on the hood of the car, as if this was where I always sat when I carpooled with the Kellys. I did a hood-ornament pose, all cool and windblown. When Mrs. Petra grabbed the dogs, I did a graceful little roll off and scrambled into the back of the van. Mrs. Petra leaned on the car door, talking to Kelly's mom. I sure hoped she was apologizing for her nasty dogs, but they were both whispering and I couldn't hear a word. I looked down glumly at the CD in my lap. The case was cracked. Not only that, my jeans were grimy from rubbing against the dirty car. I wished I could go home and start all over again — or not start at all.

Mrs. O'Brien made a U-turn and flicked a glance at me in the rearview mirror. "Are you afraid of dogs, Lindy?" she asked.

I could hardly get enough breath to answer. I was squeezed between an infant seat and a booster seat. All the little Kellys were staring at me like I was some kind of escaped rare animal from the zoo. "No, ma'am," I managed to answer. "I am not afraid of dogs. I am afraid of those monsters you just saw. They're not like real dogs. They are vicious man-eaters."

Kelly laughed. "You're so funny, Lindy."

I noticed that she was wearing makeup. She smelled kind of perfumy, too. I wondered with a sudden panic whether I had remembered to put on my deodorant. It was hard to tell. One of the little Kellys had done something in his diaper and the smell in the backseat was pretty bad. I hoped the odor didn't stick to me after I got out of the car.

When we pulled up to Eric's house, I thought I was going to throw up. I started to really miss Andy Carlucci and his family's little apartment on Allegheny Avenue. Maybe Andy bragged a lot, but I knew he was no better than me, and I never felt sick like this when I went to visit him. His apartment wasn't much different than the little row house my family rented on the next block. It had everything a person could ever need: a living room with a TV, a kitchen, a bathroom, and a few bedrooms. Andy and I usually hung out on a couple of deflated beanbag chairs and played video games. I thought we were normal.

Eric's house was like something Andy and I would gape at on a TV show. Real people didn't live there. Movie stars and millionaires did, but certainly not the kid who sat behind you in English class. Tall trees and flowerbeds lined the whole driveway, all the way up to the front door, and I kept expecting a band to pop out and play something presidential. The house was huge, with big white columns in the front, kind of like the White House. Not that I've ever been to the White House, but I think Eric's place is definitely bigger. It even had its own name, Eagle's View.

Maybe I'd get Dad to make a fancy sign for our house — Roadkill Estate. I sucked in my breath and climbed out of the car. I didn't belong here. I really didn't belong here. Pretty soon, somebody was going to find me out.

"Thank you for the ride, Mrs. O'Brien," I called as she pulled away.

I swallowed hard. "Kelly, we cannot go in there."

"What are you talking about?" She skipped up the steps.

"Kelly," I hissed, "wouldn't you like to just go hang out in the woods over there? I mean, you like nature, right? Squirrels are a lot more interesting than some of those kids we go to school with. C'mon, Kel, it'll be fun." I briefly thought about running after Mrs. O'Brien's car and clinging to the back bumper, but Kelly grabbed my arm and dragged me to the front door. The butler probably wouldn't let me in anyway. He'd know right away that I was an imposter. I've seen that happen in the movies lots of times.

But it was Eric's mom who answered the door. "Hello, Kelly! How are you? Come on in. Who's your friend?" Eric's mom was thin and blond. She had a movie-star smile and diamonds in her ears. She looked like the kind of person who did TV commercials for really expensive cars — you know, the kind where the husband and wife come out of some fancy restaurant and they love their car so much that they take the long way home through the winding mountain road, even though it's fifteen hours out of their way.

"Hi, Mrs. Crosby. This is Lindy. She's new to our school this year." Kelly slid off her clogs and put them in the pile of shoes by the door.

I felt the first bead of sweat pop out of my right underarm. I wasn't exactly careful about the socks I wore. The invitation didn't say anything about this being a socks-only party. Why had all the kids taken off their shoes?

Mrs. Crosby stared at my feet. "Oh yes. Hello, Lindy. Eric's told me all about you."

Kelly poked me. "Lindy, your shoes!"

"Oh, yeah. Sorry," I mumbled. I turned my back and kicked them off. Rats. I had a hole in my right sock just over the big toe. I tried to squeeze the threads together, but of course they didn't stay.

Mrs. Crosby's shoes clicked across the marble foyer. How come she was allowed to have footwear? This must be some kind of strange suburban custom I don't know anything about. Kelly and I padded after her. I felt like shouting "helloooo" up toward the cavernous ceiling to see if there would be an echo. Maybe the chandelier would shake and fall on my head. Everyone would feel so sorry for me. I'd have to spend months and months in the hospital watching TV. Eric would send flowers every day, and Mrs. Tremont would cry beside my bed, begging me to forgive her rudeness. And when Mom and Dad visited, I would finally tell them about Rebecca and what I did. They wouldn't even get mad. They would just pat my hand and tell me to get well, that all was forgiven.

"Lindy?" Kelly was halfway down the hall.

"I'm coming," I mumbled. The chandelier was still attached to the ceiling. So I threw back my shoulders and strutted after Kelly. I acted cool, like I had a foyer at home and it was just like this. I wonder what people use them for. I wish I could ask somebody.

"They're just out back there on the deck," Mrs. Crosby said. "Lindy, hon, would you mind taking that tray out with you, the one on the island?"

Wow. Their kitchen had an island that was so big that at least two people could camp out on it. I picked up a heavy platter filled with some kind of crackery things.

Kelly pulled open the sliding door and waited for me. I sucked in my breath and stepped outside. I tried to keep my left foot forward and hoped no one would see the hole in my right sock.

"Oh, look!" Melissa cried. "The server is here." She snapped her fingers at me. "Bring me a few, girl. Hurry up now."

Everyone stared. I wanted to give her a few — right up her nose.

Eric hurried over. "Hey, thanks for coming, Lindy," he said. "Hey, Kelly."

"Hey," Kelly answered. She turned back and winked at me.

My palms were all sweaty and, for some reason, the tray had gained about twenty pounds since I came outside. But at least it kept Eric from being able to look straight down at the hole in my sock.

"Want me to take that?"

"No. I'm OK with it," I insisted. "I'll just carry it around in case anybody wants some of these, um . . . whatever they are." I imagined myself holding onto the tray for the whole party, using it as a shield so that nobody could get a good view of my holey sock.

Eric laughed. "I don't know what they are, either. One of my mom's new creations, I guess. Let me put it down on the table over there and you can grab something to eat."

"No, no, I'm fine with it."

"No, let me take it." As we struggled over the tray, Eric's fingers got tangled up with mine. He gave me a small smile and I pulled away.

"Here, this is for you," I quickly said. "I was sort of hiding it under the tray since I didn't have time to wrap it. And I accidentally dropped it when I was getting into Kelly's car, so the case is kind of cracked. I hope it's OK. Happy birthday."

"Cool! It's just what I wanted. This is awesome." He set the tray down and pretended to be engrossed in the song titles on the back of the CD.

"Nice wrapping paper." Melissa had sidled up to Eric and was picking at a bowl of Cheese Doodles.

"Yeah, well, we ran out of paper." I put my left foot over my right and leaned against the table.

"Where'd you buy it? I heard they're hard to get." Melissa chewed with her mouth open and I could see her tongue turning orange.

"Music Town, of course." There was no way I was going to tell her about Freddy. The less she knew about me the better. Music Town is a popular store in the mall where a lot of kids hang out on Saturday nights flipping through the CDs. You can even listen to your favorite songs on the headphones at the end of each aisle. I was in there once with Freddy while Mom was buying Randy some shoes a couple of stores away.

"Really?" Melissa drawled. "At Music Town they wrap for free." She paused for effect. "Unless, of course, you leave the store without *paying*. Some poor people do that."

"I wouldn't know since I always *pay* for things," I spat. "By the way, how'd you get that orange stuff all over your face?"

"What?" Melissa touched her fingers to each cheek. Her face had been perfectly clean, but now she had orange fingerprints smeared into her makeup. What a dope.

Eric chuckled.

“What?” Melissa whipped around at him.

“Nothing, nothing.” Eric put both hands up in front of himself. “I just gotta go talk to Kyle and Matt.” He abandoned me. I looked around desperately for Kelly, but she was giggling away at some story Kyle was telling.

“You think you’re so smart, Lindy,” Melissa sputtered, wiping her face with a napkin.

“Smarter than you anyway.” I took a long sip of my soda.

“Yeah? Well, we’ll see. I had a basketball tournament this weekend, and I ran into your good friend Morgan.”

“Good for you.” I stuck the Coke can up to my mouth, but I only pretended to drink. My throat closed up when I heard Morgan’s name and I was afraid I might choke.

“I asked her if she knew you, and she said yes. If her mom wasn’t hanging over her shoulder, we could have talked some.”

“What a shame.” I relaxed a little and managed a swallow of soda.

“Yeah, well, we exchanged e-mail addresses. She’s going to write to me. Maybe she’s writing something to me right now.”

My heart dropped down to my stomach. I kept my face blank, though, so she wouldn’t know I was concerned. “Wonderful,” I drawled. “Maybe you’ll finally make a friend.”

Eric’s dad was flipping burgers on a grill that was twice the size of the oven in our kitchen. Everybody crowded around with their plates.

"Plain or cheese?" he asked when I had made it to the front of the line. Mr. Crosby had the same smooth hair as Eric, only it was white and didn't hang so far down his forehead. He had those crinkly lines around his eyes that made it look as if he was always smiling. I guess that if you lived in a house like this, you probably woke up every day with a smile and laughed yourself to sleep every night.

"Cheese would be great. Thank you."

He plopped the burger onto my plate. "I don't think we've ever met."

"Oh, sorry, Dad," Eric said. "This is Lindy Perkins. She's new to our school this year."

Mr. Crosby did a little bow in his chef's apron. "Pleased to meet you, Lindy Perkins." He flipped a plain burger onto Eric's plate. "How do you like it at Mecong?"

"Good," I mumbled through a mouthful of burger.

"Where're you from?" he asked.

I took a moment to chew and to swallow what was in my mouth. And to think. "Oh, I'm from . . . uh . . . California." I've never actually been to California, but I know it's a big state and it's really far from Pennsylvania.

"I thought you said you were from Idaho," Kelly blurted. She and Kyle were sitting in matching white rockers.

I shot her a piercing glance.

"But maybe I got it wrong," she quickly added.

"No, you're right, Kel. I was . . . I was from Idaho. That was before we moved to California." I could feel a moistness spreading in my armpits. I pressed my arms to my sides, locking it in.

"California, land of the sun," Mr. Crosby sang. "I spent a number of years there myself. Where about did you live?"

"Oh, right around the middle somewhere. We lived in Santa . . . Santa Clausio."

Mr. Crosby's eyebrows went up a little bit, but he didn't say anything.

"Santa Clausio?" Melissa snorted. "I've been to California about ten times and I never heard of any Santa Clausio."

I narrowed my eyes. "It's a big state, Melissa. Have you been to every single town?" I looked up at Mr. Crosby. "Santa Clausio is small and not too many people have heard of it, but it's real pretty."

Melissa opened her mouth, but nothing came out. I think that's the first time that ever happened. I was feeling more confident by the minute.

Mr. Crosby squirted ketchup onto his burger. "So what brings you to the East Coast?"

Couldn't we get off this subject? Kelly and Kyle were trying to secretly hold hands. Couldn't we make fun of them or of Matt's acne, or gossip about kids who weren't here? Couldn't we just talk about normal twelve-year-old stuff? Everyone was staring at me, waiting. I took a deep breath. "Well, you see, my dad is this . . . like . . . engineer, and he built all kinds of stuff for Hollywood movies when we were in Santa Clausio. And it was fun and all in the beginning, you know, seeing all those movie stars every day. But he got kind of bored building pretend things for movies and he wanted to do some real building."

"You saw movie stars?! You're so lucky," Gabby gushed. "Did you get any autographs?"

"Wait a minute. Your dad wants to do some real building in Shelbourne?" Melissa sneered. "Give me a break."

"Well, all over the area. You know, in Philadelphia and New York."

"Really? Is he part of that local firm that . . . , " Mr. Crosby began.

"Lindy's a great athlete, Dad," Eric interrupted. "She hits a home run practically every game she's in at school. She's close to breaking a school record."

"Yeah," Kelly said. "She might do it on Monday. We have our first playoff game against Pennswood. You only need two more to break the record, right, Lindy?"

I shrugged. "I don't know. I guess." It was definitely two. I was keeping track by scratching hash marks into the wall beside my bed. At first I scratched them into my arm with a pin, but my mom got all freaked out.

"That's terrific." Mr. Crosby nodded at me. "You should get Lindy to give you a few tips, Eric."

"I know," Eric said.

"Excuse me. I'll be right back." I turned and limped to the house. It gets really painful after a while with one foot standing on the other one. I could barely feel my toes. I had to do something about the hole in my sock.

I opened a couple of closets and a pantry before I found the bathroom. I locked myself inside. I sat on the toilet lid and pulled at my hair. Morgan would surely tell Melissa that I lived in the shelter, and Melissa would spread the word all around school. I had to think of some kind of plan. I was sweating a lot and it wasn't even that hot. It had to be this bathroom. It made me feel as if I were trapped in some weird window display in a beach store. There were seashell towels hanging from a sailboat rack. To turn the light on, you had to push a button inside a striped lighthouse. There were sea gulls with beady eyes perched on a shelf above the toilet. Next to them was a flickering dolphin candle.

I felt a little self-conscious with the sea gulls staring at me, but I did a quick check of my underarms. They were damp, but at least I didn't smell too bad. I dipped my finger in a little of the dolphin's wax and pressed it on the inside of my shirt. Now I should have the aroma of an ocean breeze. At least that's what the sticker on the bottom of the candle said.

I pulled off my sock. I turned it around and slid it on backward. The heel made a big lump on the top of my foot, and you could still see the hole anyway. The heck with it. I'd just go barefoot. I tried to stuff the socks in my pockets, but they made too big of a bulge. I stood up straight and looked at myself in the crab-shaped mirror above the sink. It is a sad fact that my nose sticks out farther than anything else on my body. Melissa has a big chest, and for some reason that I cannot understand, this makes her popular. Without her chest, I bet everybody else would hate her as much as I do. I took the balled-up socks and fitted them under my shirt, one at a time.

Maybe it could work for me, too. I turned to look at my profile. It was a little lumpy, but I liked it.

There was a knock at the door and I jumped. "Just a minute! I'll be right out." I flushed the toilet even though I didn't do anything in it. After one last look, I pulled the socks out of my shirt. I wasn't brave enough to go through with it. I wrapped the socks in a big wad of toilet paper and stuffed them in the bottom of the starfish trash can.

Gabby was waiting outside the door and slipped past me into the bathroom. "Hey, Lindy. Grab your shoes. Everybody's going out to the basketball court."

"What?"

"Basketball. Hurry up."

I stared longingly at the starfish trash can that held my now-necessary socks. While I was thinking about how to get them back, Gabby clicked the door shut. Two minutes late again. The cold marble floor on my bare feet sent a chill up my spine. I went to find my shoes.

ERIC WHIPPED THE BALL AT ME. I did a quick spin dribble and took a jump shot. It swished. This court was beautiful, surrounded by the rolling green hills of Bucks County, and it belonged just to Eric. I thought of the basketball court off Allegheny Avenue that my dad had taken me to as soon as I was able to walk. Sometimes we had to sweep the broken glass off the asphalt before we could even play. But it was worth it. He taught me V-cuts and jump stops and pick-and-rolls. We played Pig or Horse. Whenever he challenged me to a one-on-one, I pretended that I was Allen Iverson up against Shaq. And he didn't let me win just because I was a kid. He had more respect for me than that. He always treated me like an equal, like one of his buddies.

My mom always said that Dad was nothing but a big overgrown kid. She wished he'd play a little less and take care of things around the house a lot more. Not me. Who cares if you have to jiggle the handle on the toilet every time you flush? And it didn't matter at all that my closet door never shut. It just made it easier to get the clothes out every day. I told that to Dad, too, when we were having our postgame Coke on a bench in the playground. I saw the way it made him smile, his head tilted back to get the sun full blast.

Dad helped me a lot, but mostly I think I perfected my shot at the homeless shelter. There was a basket in the parking lot out back with a chain link net. I used to shoot there for hours at a time. I could get into a rhythm where my whole mind was focused on the ball going in the net and I could block out any thoughts of my family just inside: my dad, lying flat out on the cot, his work boots that didn't work anymore poking out at the end; my mom, thin and pale in the fluorescent light, squinting at the newspaper, always searching for some sort of job that she could do; Randy, his left thumb in his mouth, his right hand curled into some piece of Mom's clothes, holding on for dear life, as though he would disappear into thin air — vanish, just like Rebecca — if he ever let go.

Freddy would come out and shoot with me sometimes, but I usually left him and went to sit on the hard ground behind a car. He always wanted me to talk about Rebecca. I just wanted to forget.

"Ball hog!" Melissa grabbed the basketball out of my hands. I had taken three more shots and made them all. Melissa backed up and buried a three. She played with some fancy AAU team and even traveled to different states to play in tournaments. She bragged about it all the time. I have to admit she was good. But when it came time for choosing teams, Eric picked me first.

"What?" Melissa spat. "You're picking her?"

Eric shrugged. "I'll pick you next." He whispered to me, "Melissa lives next door. She hangs out here sometimes."

Next door? My eyes searched the horizon. I could just make out the tip of a brick chimney beyond the trees. In the city, next door meant that if you drilled a hole in your wall and stuck your fist through, you could shake hands with your neighbor. You knew what TV shows they watched, which days they practiced the piano, and every detail about the fights they were having. In the homeless shelter, you didn't even have a wall between neighbors, just about six inches of air space. Melissa didn't live next door. She practically lived in the next county. I wished I could send her back.

Colin picked Melissa before Eric could. So at least we were on opposite teams. That was appropriate. I could feel my feet sweating already into the hard soles of my shoes. If I didn't kill everybody with my basketball skills, I would definitely knock them out with my foot odor.

We decided the first possession by a flip of the coin. Ben inbounded to Melissa, and I pressed her all the way up the court. She was showing off, dribbling behind her back and through her legs. Some of the kids watching from the side were oohing and aahing. I went for the steal and she blew past me down the lane. Kelly left her man to help out, which meant that Colin was wide open under the basket. But Melissa ignored him and took the shot herself. She made it.

"And one!" Melissa yelled, pumping her fist in the air.

"Forget about it," Kyle argued.

Melissa poked Kelly in the shoulder. "She was all over me. What are you talking about? I practically have a bruise here from where she hit me."

"Oh, give it a break, Melissa." Kyle gripped the ball.

"Let her take it, Kyle." Eric grabbed the ball and flipped it to Melissa. "We'll get it back."

I stood at half-court and everybody else, including Ben who should have been covering me, stood at the lane. Just as Melissa was about to release, Kyle screamed "box out" at the top of his lungs. Melissa flinched, and the shot was off. Eric jumped for the rebound as I raced for our basket all alone. Eric thew the ball down court to me, and I laid it in. Piece of cake.

"Ben! Will you please play defense?" Melissa yelled. "Are you confused about your position or what?"

"I thought you were covering Lindy," Ben complained.

"How can I cover her when I'm on the foul line!? Wake up, would you?"

I leaned toward Eric. "Now I know why you didn't pick her for your team," I whispered.

Eric smiled. "She's all right. She's just real serious about her basketball."

We were playing to twenty, each basket counting for one, except threes, which were worth two. I took the first three-pointer and made it. Melissa charged up court and made a three on her next possession. She smirked at me. I hated to admit it while I was dribbling down the court — Melissa's red, sweaty face right in mine — but she was better than me. I thought I could shoot just as well, but Melissa had moves that faked me out big time.

I drove the lane, faked a shot, and passed to Kelly underneath. She wasn't expecting the pass. She fumbled with the ball for a second, then threw up a wild shot. "Sorry, everybody!" she called.

"Don't worry about it." I ran backward, keeping my eye on the ball.

Colin picked it up and threw the outlet to Melissa. It was hard playing in jeans, and my feet were sloshing around inside my shoes. Otherwise, I might have kept up with her. She faked left and went right and made a beautiful shot from the top of the key. I was giving up more points than I was scoring. When Melissa dribbled, the ball was practically a part of her body. I couldn't do that, and she must have stolen the ball off me about six times.

Eric was good, too, a natural. I liked to watch him move to the basket, long and lean, jump straight up, and kiss the ball against the backboard. But Melissa was too much for us. We lost, 20–15.

For one teeny, tiny moment, though, we almost forgot that we hated each other. "Nice game," Melissa said to me.

"Yeah, you, too. You were pretty awesome."

"Thanks." She sat in the grass and ran her fingers through her hair. "I play a lot. You on a team?"

"No."

"You have some potential. You should check out my club, the Renegades. They might have an opening for a B player like you."

Kelly bounced over and flopped on the ground beside us. "Wow, I am so exhausted from that game." She waved her hand, fanning her freckled face.

Melissa rolled her eyes.

"Eric has the coolest house," Kelly sighed, "doesn't he?"

"It's OK," Melissa droned. "But my house has a bigger pool, and we have a tennis court, too."

"Yeah, but it's got you living in it, which reduces it to a B-quality house." I slid my shoes off and buried my burning feet in the long, cool grass.

Melissa stood and flipped her long, silky hair over her shoulder. "You're just a sore loser. At least in my house we have enough quality to wear socks." And she strode off, grass clippings stuck to the back of her legs.

"Oh my God, Lindy," Kelly gasped. "You're bleeding!"

I looked at my feet. Both of my little toes were missing some skin and were oozing blood. I quickly slid my shoes back on. "It's nothing, Kel," I assured her. And it wasn't. I don't mind that kind of pain so much. It only lasts for a little while and then it goes away. It doesn't stick inside you forever.

Eric grasped my hand and pulled me to my feet. "We're going to . . . "

Melissa jumped between us. "Lindy and I will be team captains," she interrupted. "I get to pick first, though, because I won the basketball game."

"What are we doing?" I asked.

"We're playing Manhunt. I pick Eric." Melissa grabbed Eric's arm and pulled him next to her.

The other kids all came to stand around us. "OK, I'll take Kelly."

Kelly smiled and jumped to my side. "Pick Kyle next," Kelly whispered.

"Why Kyle?"

"'Cause he's cute," she giggled.

Melissa chose Matt and I picked Kyle, even though being cute is not exactly a helpful quality when playing Manhunt. The choosing went on until everyone was on a team.

"This tree is jail," Eric called. "There's no base."

I had played Manhunt about ten thousand times, and I knew that jail was where you put captured players, and I knew that most times you played without a base, or a safe spot. But the rules in the city were that you had to stick to your block, which included both streets and the alley in back. No crossing the street or going in any house or basement was allowed. We hid behind trash cans and parked cars and raced down the alley and up on the cement patios out front. All they had here was one giant house and a whole lot of woods. And since it was getting dark, I wasn't so sure I even wanted to go in there.

"Kel," I whispered, "is there any out-of-bounds or anything?"

"No," she cried. "You better run!"

The other team had started counting and we only had up to twenty to get away. Everyone took off toward the woods and I followed. I knew Melissa would hunt me down first, and I wasn't about to let her beat me in basketball and Manhunt in the same day. I figured I would go into the woods and make a loop back toward the other side of the house. Maybe I could find some comfortable landscaping to hide in. I was tired of running. Every step I took rubbed a little more skin off my toes. It felt like I was down to the bone.

I heard my teammates crunching through the undergrowth.

"Lindy!" Kelly hissed. "This way!"

"No," I called back. "I have a plan. Come with me."

The enemy had finished counting and was racing toward the woods. Kelly waved her arms and disappeared into the darkness. Great. I plunged through some bushes and across a small clearing and climbed over a bunch of rocks. I stopped a minute to catch my breath and to make sure that I still had ten toes. I was safe. The shouts of the kids were getting farther and farther away.

I suddenly noticed that it was really creepy in these woods. What if there were bears out here or something? I hoped I was going the right way. I'd give anything to be sitting on my old front stoop right now, warm cement against my skin, neighbors' voices drifting all around me, Rebecca chalking up the sidewalk.

Sometimes, I think I see her. It happened a lot at the shelter. Some little kid would pop up from between the beds. I'd see a flash of yellow hair, and a jolt of excitement would flash through me. There she is! But it wasn't ever her. I'd see Mom watching me sometimes, as if she knew what I was just thinking. She would come over and try to put her arm around me. I would run outside and shoot baskets. When you've done something bad, it only makes you feel worse to have people who don't know what you did feeling sorry for you. It would be a whole lot better if Mom would give up trying to console me. I wish she would just knock me in the head and insist that I tell the truth. But then, she doesn't know that I'm hiding anything. I still see Rebecca — sometimes in a passing car, sometimes in the crowded Wal-Mart. But I don't tell anybody.

"I'm sorry, Rebecca." I said it to the woods. "I'm sorry, Rebecca." I said it louder up to the leaves and the sky. I had this weird feeling like she was here, over my shoulder somewhere, following me. I kept turning around real fast, but I couldn't see anything. It was so dark. It never got this dark in the city. They needed some kind of lights out here. I hated the woods. I hated the suburbs. I sat in the dirt and leaned up against a big, fat tree. I didn't have a clue where I was anymore. Everything looked the same.

Something was moving up ahead of me. "Rebecca?" I froze. Why didn't I just go with Kelly? "Who's there?" I squeaked. It froze, too, and stared at me. I slowly got to my feet. Not more than five yards away was one of those big deer with antler things on its head. Frantically, I looked all around me. I saw a tree with boards nailed to it and I made a dash for it. I climbed the boards up onto a little wooden platform. The deer was butting its head up against a little tree nearby. I made it just in time. I sat real still and prayed that it would go away.

"Lin-deee!" It sounded like Eric. I sat up straight. The deer stopped attacking the tree and looked up, too.

"Come out, you idiot!" That was definitely Melissa. I'd know her screech anywhere. The deer ran away, its white tail flashing through the darkness.

"The game is over!" Melissa yelled. "We give up. You win. Now come out." They were practically right beneath me now.

"She's just doing this for the attention, you know," Melissa complained. "I'm not going to look for her all night. She'll come out eventually."

"Maybe she's lost," Eric insisted.

"Lost? Even Lindy can't be that stupid. She just always has to be the center of attention. She's so annoying." Melissa picked up a stick and started whacking it against the very tree I was sitting in. I had an urge to jump out of the tree right onto her head, just like in an old cowboy-and-Indian movie. But Eric was there, so I sat like a statue.

"Lay off her," Eric said.

"Why should I? I don't know why you like her anyway. She's such a jerk."

"I think she's pretty cool. She's funny and all."

"She isn't funny. You don't know anything about her, Eric. Everything she says is a lie. Didn't you ever notice that? I mean, why does she have to lie all the time? And her clothes! Where does she get those things?"

I looked down at my jeans and Francine's old striped shirt. They were ugly — even in the dark. If only my face were pretty or my hair, it wouldn't be so bad. I pulled at a string that was hanging from my shirt. I couldn't figure out why Eric liked me, either.

"Why don't you go back," Eric suggested. "I'll just look for five more minutes and then I'll give up, too. You're probably right. She'll come out if she thinks we stopped looking for her."

"Fine. I'm getting eaten alive out here, and I'm not wasting one more second of my life on Lindy Perkins." Melissa slapped at a few bugs and headed back the way she had come.

Eric stood quietly under the tree. I never knew the woods could be so noisy. Things I couldn't see were chirping and clicking and humming all around me. I hoped none of them were poisonous. I sure didn't want to get stuck spending the whole night out here. I wanted to be found. I cleared my throat a few times.

"I thought so!" Eric climbed the makeshift ladder and swung up onto the platform.

"Hey," he said.

"Hey," I answered sheepishly.

Eric sat cross-legged beside me. "This is a cool spot. I come here sometimes. I thought you would probably find it."

I didn't think it was cool at all, but I kept quiet. Sure it was high up, but mostly it was just creepy. I wished I could show Eric the roof of our old row house in Philadelphia. Now that was really cool. When Mom wasn't around, sometimes Dad and I would go out the upstairs window and climb onto the flat black-tar roof. We'd lie on our backs and stare up at the sky, no trees to block our view, no one to bother us. And Dad would tell me stories. He would say, "Give me three things." And I could answer, "A fish, a mountain, and a piece of string." Then he would manage to put them all together into the most amazing story.

Dad hasn't told a single story since Rebecca left us. Maybe if we could get back to that roof somehow, just for a few hours. When he asked me to give him three things, I would say, "Rebecca, a magazine, and two minutes." There's a piece of that story that even Dad doesn't know. If we were up on that roof, maybe I could I tell it.

Eric retied his shoe. "Were you hiding up here?" he asked.

"Sort of. Nobody came this way and it was boring. I was just sitting by that tree and a big deer came after me, so I climbed up here."

Eric smiled at me, his eyes bright even in the darkness.

"What? What's so funny?"

"It came after you?"

"Well, it could have. It had big, sharp antlers, and I don't have anything to defend myself."

Eric was still smiling at me, that smooth hair of his falling just into his eyes. Melissa was right about one thing: Eric didn't know anything about me. I didn't know anything about him, either. Can you like someone just because of his smile and the way his hair falls into his eyes?

"We should probably get back," Eric said.

"Yeah, OK."

He climbed down first and I followed. "Is this a tree house that you made?" I asked.

"Tree house? No. It's an old hunter's platform. The hunter sits up there and shoots the deer."

"So the deer are dangerous!" I exulted.

"No!" Eric gave me a little shove in the shoulder, like I was putting him on.

I was so confused. A big animal with sharp things on its head isn't dangerous. But if it's not dangerous, why do they shoot it? I was never going to figure out the suburbs.

"I think the hunter should have to wear antlers and butt heads with the deer. That would be more fair."

Eric laughed. "I would totally like to watch that."

We walked back slowly through the woods. They weren't as creepy when you had someone to walk with. And it did smell good, like pinecones and Christmas trees, all sweet and green.

Eric stopped suddenly and turned toward me. "Lindy? Do you want to be my girlfriend?"

A gust of wind blew through the trees and swirled past us, rippling Eric's shirt. I didn't want to say no, but I wasn't sure what yes meant. "Well . . . I guess . . . yeah," I finally stuttered.

"Good. That's so cool."

We started walking again. I was Eric's girlfriend! I liked the way that sounded, but it scared me a little, too. Andy Carlucci from Philadelphia was my friend and he was a boy, but he was never my boyfriend. I know there's a difference, but I didn't exactly understand it.

The wind was swirling through the trees now and the air had the faint smell of rain. It felt like a storm was coming, but the sky was so dark it was hard to tell. Eric walked with his head down and I thought that maybe he realized he had made a big mistake asking me to be his girlfriend. He stopped and looked at me. He was wearing cargo pants and a big navy T-shirt with a white stripe across the chest. The stripe stood out in the dark. "We should make it official," he announced, taking my hands. "OK?"

"Yeah. OK." I thought maybe we were going to carve our initials into one of the trees or prick our fingers.

But Eric leaned toward me and we stood motionless for a minute, the wind whipping between us like it does through the crevice in my bedroom wall. And then it was gone, sealed. Eric's face was right up against mine. I squeezed my eyes closed and he kissed me. It was real fast and he sort of missed, just kissing the side of my mouth. But it did feel more official than cutting your finger with an old knife. I hoped I didn't have cheeseburger breath.

We walked back real slowly, not saying anything. The trees were thrashing about way above us and the air was turning cooler. I could make out the lights from Eric's house ahead.

There was a big fallen tree just in front of us. Eric climbed on the trunk and took my hand, pulling me up. We stood there for a moment looking out toward his empty backyard, his hand still in mine.

"I remember the first day you came to Mecong," he said.

I felt my face burn. It wasn't my greatest day.

"I never saw a girl punch like that before," Eric said. "It was awesome. And Brandon must be, like, six inches taller than you."

I was pretty nervous that first day. And this kid Brandon was following me down the hall after classes, making fun of me. I was handling it OK until he poked me in the shoulder. I figured I better get him before he got me. I swung around, my fist clenched, and hit him square in the face. I must have opened a vein in his nose, because he was squirting blood everywhere. All the kids in the hall looked at me like I was one of those crazy school shooters. I picked up my books and headed for the door. But I didn't make it. Mr. Hambley, the P.E. teacher, grabbed me by the back of the neck and pushed me down the hall into the principal's office. After that, they made me go to regular meetings with the fat school psychologist. Like I would ever tell her anything.

"I didn't know you were there that day," I stammered. "I was a little nervous. I don't do that stuff anymore."

"I just think it's cool how you stick up for yourself and your little brother."

"Randy."

"Yeah. Randy. He's a cute kid."

"He's real smart," I bragged. "And he's a genius with puzzles. He just loves them."

"He was talking to me a mile a minute at your game last week. He told me you have an older brother, too, and a little sister. But he said that she was lost or something. I couldn't really figure out what he saying. What was that all about?" Eric laughed, as if there was some cute, easy explanation for Randy's mixed-up story.

I felt my insides cramp up. What happened to Rebecca is one puzzle that Randy just can't seem to solve even though it was explained to him about one thousand times. There was a flash of lightning across the sky and it lit up the trees towering all around us. A low, growling thunder rumbled in the distance. I felt Eric's eyes on me, waiting. I didn't know what to say. A gust of wind brought down a spray of cold rain on us and I screamed. We jumped from the tree and ran for the house, Eric's question hanging unanswered in the woods behind us.

16

◆ ◆ ◆

On May 23, I rolled out of bed early and pushed open the window. It almost didn't seem fair. It was a beautiful day, bright and warm. Even the clouds of exhaust floating up from the highway couldn't completely extinguish that fresh spring smell in the air. For a second, I thought about what it would be like to jump in front of one of those tractor-trailers. I leaned way out the window and tried to see into the yard. I wondered how Dad was handling it. As of today, Rebecca has been gone for one whole year.

I crept downstairs. Mom and Freddy were at the kitchen table, hunched over their coffee, whispering. Lit candles of every color and size were set up all over the place. There were three on the table in front of Mom, two on the counter, three scattered around the living room, one on the bottom step, and a skinny yellow one squeezed onto the window ledge.

When I saw the coffee table, I thought I was dreaming. I steadied myself against the banister and just stared. Then I moved silently toward it, a numbness stealing over my body. Two more candles, set in little glass jars, were burning in front of a framed photo of Rebecca. It was the one we had taken in Sears, the one where I had pretended to trip and fall on the floor over and over again so she would laugh for the photographer. The giggle picture — that's what Dad called it. And all around it somebody had arranged her toys. I thought that Mom had given them all away, but here were the floating bathtub animals, the little yellow school bus, the stacking cups. Next to them lay her babydoll, sleeping peacefully on the glass-topped table, as though Rebecca had just left it there for a minute and gone off to play.

I dropped to my knees. Where did this stuff come from? Rebecca loved that doll. They should have let her keep it. Why didn't they let her keep it? I fingered the doll's plastic hands, curled into tight little fists. I touched its soft, pajamaed body and stared at the brown juice stain on its left leg. I remembered when Rebecca did that. I sat the baby up. The eyes popped open and stared at me. "Maamaa," it wailed.

I dropped the doll and jumped to my feet, suddenly angry. "What is this?" I demanded.

"Oh, sweetheart." Mom looked up, startled. Her eyes were dark and puffy. "Come sit with us."

I didn't want to sit. I paced between the kitchen and the living room, looking at all the half-burnt candles.

"What is this?" I asked again.

"I don't know, honey. Dad must have set it up early this morning. It was here when I got in from work."

And then suddenly I remembered. I ran from the kitchen to the living room and then back. I counted twice to make sure. Twelve. There were twelve candles. My knees felt all wobbly.

"Lindy, stop," Freddy said. "Come and sit down here. Come on."

"There are twelve candles," I said. "Twelve." But they wouldn't understand what it meant. Only Dad would. It was one of his rooftop stories. An Indian, a candle, a kidnapping. A girl was stolen by the Indians out on the frontier. Her dad was a candlemaker. Every month that she was gone, he lit another candle on the anniversary of her disappearance. After several years, his house was bright with the flames. The legend of the glowing house grew and his story spread far and wide, even to the Indians themselves. One dark night, when his house was lit like a beacon, his daughter found her way home. Dad's stories always ended happily. I had to find him.

I ran to the door and flung it open. "Dad!" I called.

"He's not there, Lindy," Freddy said quietly. "We already checked."

I jumped off the porch and into the yard. Dad's latest trash sculpture was in pieces. I leaned against the fence and banged my head on the wood. The vibrations of the morning rush-hour traffic trembled down my back. Why hadn't I ever told him that it was my fault, that I had heard him calling me loud and clear, but I just didn't come? Why didn't I ever explain what I did? What was wrong with me? I bit down hard on the inside of my cheek. Warm, salty blood spread across my tongue. But it didn't help.

Mom was coming down the porch steps after me. "Lindy," she beckoned, her arms out to hold me. "Come here."

"Where is he?" I asked, ignoring her arms. "Where is he?"

"I don't know. It is trash day," she offered, leaning against the fence next to me. "He's probably out looking for things. Are you OK?"

Freddy had come out onto the porch. He stood there in his worn-out jeans with the hole in the knee, running his hand through his overgrown hair and staring at me.

"I'm perfectly fine. Stop fussing over me!"

I saw the look Mom gave to Freddy. My hands were clenched and I was breathing fast. I just wanted Dad to be here.

"C'mon, Lindy," Freddy urged. "Come and sit with Mom and me. You can even try the coffee. Can't she, Mom?"

"I hate coffee," I screamed at him.

"Lindy . . . ," Mom began.

I pulled away from her. I just ran. I pushed through the shrubbery, branches scratching at my arms and pulling my hair. I stayed close to the highway. I found a spot where the fence was loose and I kicked at it over and over until a small piece gave way and crumbled onto the shoulder of the bypass. I squeezed through.

"DAD!" I screamed. "DAD!" But the rushing traffic swallowed up my voice, and I couldn't see him anywhere.

I stood in the gravel and the dirt at the side of the road, litter swirling at my feet. The trucks smacked me with great gusts of air as they flew by. It stung my eyes and took my breath away. I stepped a little closer.

"Lindy!" Freddy had followed me, but he was too big to fit through the hole I had made. I heard him kicking at the fence. "He's not out there! I swear I looked. I drove all around before you woke up."

I looked down at the white line just in front of my feet. A big tractor-trailer sounded its horn at me, long and hard. I felt the power of its wheels crunching just inches from me and the rumble of its engine in my chest. I could have touched it. The swirl of exhaust and dust filled my lungs.

"C'mon, Lindy!" Freddy screamed. "You're getting Mom upset!"

I stood for a minute between the highway and the fence, watching the traffic fly south. I thought of that dead cat. If I got hit, would they brush my hair and put me under the hubcap tree?

Freddy was still screaming at me from the other side of the fence. "Lindy! Come back! What are you doing out there?"

I didn't know. I really didn't know. I heard a crack, and a piece of the fence flopped onto the shoulder. Freddy stuck his head through and stared at me.

"Are you crazy?" he asked. He wasn't screaming anymore, but his face was all red. "Think about Mom, would you? Please, come on back home now."

But I just stood there looking south, feeling the pull of the retreating cars and trucks. Freddy finally squeezed through the fence and came to stand beside me. He put his hand on my shoulder, but I pushed it off.

"Lindy, are you OK?"

I didn't answer him. He tried to take my hand, but I pulled away. I didn't need his help. I crawled back through the hole on my own and marched toward home.

Mom was rocking on the porch, Randy curled on her lap. She stood up and reached for me.

"Lindy . . ."

"I have to get ready for school," I said.

She was standing in front of the door, blocking me. "Stay home today, sweetheart. It's OK. I called in sick. I'll stay with you."

I didn't want to stay home and have Mom fuss over me all day. I needed to hit something. I needed to play softball. I needed to stand at the plate and forget everything in the whole world except for the ball flying toward me.

So even though it felt like there was a knife stuck in my throat, cutting me with every breath I took, I swallowed hard and kept my voice calm and even. "I'm OK, Mom," I said. "I'd really rather go to school. I have a big softball game today and I've been looking forward to playing in it."

"Are you sure?" She didn't look convinced.

"I'm sure." I gave her a quick hug for reassurance and moved her away from the door. I hurried into the house.

The picture and the toys were gone. Someone had blown out all the candles.

17

◆ ◆ ◆

I SAT AT MY DESK and stared out the window in homeroom. I'm glad that even though I know the day, I don't remember which two minutes of the day it happened. If I did, I'd probably fall right out of my seat onto the floor when they came. It would be too awful to watch them pass, to feel how quickly they slipped by.

Derrick twisted around in his seat. "Hey, Lindy," he sneered. "Or should I say, Santy Claus? I heard you grew up in Santa Clausio. Get much snow there? I guess you had to travel around in a sleigh, huh?" I watched his ugly nostrils flare as he laughed.

Melissa is wearing me out. She told everyone that I lied about Santa Clausio. Just my luck that there is no such place. I made up some pretty good excuses, though. At lunch yesterday, I explained that Santa Clausio isn't an official town, it's really just a neighborhood in Santa Barbara. But I don't care anymore. From what I hear,

Melissa and Morgan are becoming best friends on the Internet. I'm sure that Melissa knows that I came from the homeless shelter in Leedstown. She hasn't told anyone yet, so she's probably planning something big. My guess is that she's going to spill the beans at today's play-off game. If we win today against Lansford Middle School, we are the league champions. It might be my last day to have any friends.

"Ho-ho-ho," Derrick sang. "Did you hear that a lot in Santa Clausio?"

"Shut up, Derrick," Kelly cut in. She was copying her math homework into my notebook.

"You better watch out, Kelly," Derrick smirked. "I heard that Lindy came to Mecong from juvenile hall. Who knows what crimes she committed before she got locked up?"

Kelly's mouth dropped open. "I can't believe you, Derrick. Why do you have to be so mean? Don't listen to him, Lindy."

I dropped my head onto my arms and tried to focus on the bit of blue sky I could see out the window. I wondered if Kelly would still like me when she found out that I lied to her about everything, from my family to my house to my old school. I thought Eric had looked at me kind of funny in the hall this morning, but I wasn't sure. Maybe I would be better off in juvenile hall. I'd fit in better there than I do here.

Derrick turned around in his seat but started to hum Christmas carols. It was a pretty dangerous thing to do for a person who had to sit with his back to me for the rest of the year. But maybe he could tell I was giving up. Melissa could. I saw it in her face all week.

Kelly put her hand on my arm. "Here." She slid my math notebook onto my desk.

"Thanks, Kel." I think I am going to miss Kelly the most after I am exposed as a fraud. She put up with all my moods and never got mad at me. Why didn't I ever trust her with the truth?

"You're not too tired for today's game, are you?" she asked.

"No way." I sat up straight in my desk and attempted a smile. I was going to go out with a bang. I had an itch powerful enough to hit one hundred home runs. I had tied the school record on Tuesday. Today, I was going to break it wide open. Melissa might get to call me shelter kid for the rest of my life, but she would have to look at my name, printed in gold letters, on the plaque hung just outside the gym. I would have that. At least I would have that.

I was late getting to the girls' locker room to change for the game. When I pushed open the door, everyone stopped talking. Gabby's face got all red, and Jo looked down at the floor. But Melissa stared straight at me with a big smile on her face.

I dragged my gear around the row of lockers, out of view, and sat on the bench. There were some muffled giggles and cleats clicking on the tile floor.

"Hey, wait, guys," Melissa called. "I've got something else to tell you, too."

I felt my body tense. I gripped the bench and hung my head.

"Guess what?" The cleats moved closer, then quieted down. "Mrs. Tremont's husband is in the Pondview Nursing Home!"

This part wasn't about me at all. But for some reason, it still felt bad, like I had caught a bowling ball with my stomach.

"Nursing home!" Gabby exclaimed.

"Mrs. Tremont's old," Jo snickered, "but not that old! How do you know her husband's there? You're making this up."

"No! I saw him! My great aunt broke her hip and she got transferred to the nursing home. My mom made me go with her to visit my aunt, and I saw Mrs. Tremont sitting in his room. He's, like, scary looking. I peeked real quick because I didn't want her to see me. She was holding his hand and talking away to him and he didn't even have his eyes open."

"I try not to listen to her, either!" Kristin cackled.

There was scattered laughter. I was bent over double, tying my laces. When I finally raised my head, I saw her. Mrs. Tremont had come in the back way and was leaning against the doorframe several lockers away from me. She just stood there, her eyes fixed on mine, and listened while the kids on the other side of the lockers kept cutting her up.

I wondered: If Melissa weren't there, would I have joined in with them, laughing at Mrs. Tremont and her sick husband? I thought about the pillow in her car and all the old fast-food wrappers in the backseat. I couldn't look at her anymore, and I dropped my eyes to the floor. When the conversation finally changed, Mrs. Tremont slowly moved away from the doorframe and walked around the lockers.

"Girls," she snapped. "Get out there and warm up. We have a big game here. Let's go."

The locker room emptied, and Mrs. Tremont retreated to her small office in the corner. I heard the squeak of her metal chair as she dropped into it. I followed her and stood in the doorway.

She looked up at me. Her glasses had slipped all the way down to the edge of her nose. She didn't bother to push them back up. "Go on out and warm up, Lindy. This is the big game."

But I didn't go. "I'm sorry, Mrs. Tremont, " I said.

She finally pushed her glasses up on her nose and gave me a sad smile. "You didn't do anything, Lindy. You don't have anything to be sorry about."

"You have no idea." I only meant to say it in my head, but the words slipped out of my mouth. I felt a catch in my throat. "Gotta go!" I slammed her office door shut behind me.

"Lindy!" I heard her call me, but I got out of there real fast. I swallowed the lump in my throat. My face felt flush and hot. What was happening to me? I would concentrate on softball. I would think about nothing but the game, about my name in gold letters on a plaque. I tried hard, but other thoughts kept getting in my way.

18

◆ ◆ ◆

"SORRY I'M LATE." Kelly squeezed onto the bench beside me just before the game was about to start. "Mr. Ainsley made me stay after to take that makeup social studies quiz. Can you believe it? I told him I had a game."

Kelly leaned forward and scanned the bleachers. As always, her whole family was there. They waved at her.

"Oh, that reminds me." Kelly zipped open her sports bag and gave me a little box wrapped in shiny paper.

"What's this?"

"Just open it." She was wiggling into her cleats but watching me out of the corner of her eye.

I love presents. I ripped the paper off and opened up the little white box. It was filled with chocolates, all in the shape of trophies. "Wow! Thanks," I said, popping one in my mouth and offering the box to her.

"My mom made them for you — you know, for tying the school record and all."

"That is so sweet." The smooth chocolate melted on my tongue but stung the cut on the inside of my cheek. I savored both sensations. I leaned forward and waved my thank-you to Mrs. O'Brien in the stands. I froze with my hand in midair. Morgan was in the stands two rows down. She gave me a mean little wave and then crossed her arms. The chocolate slipped down my throat the wrong way and I went into a spasm of coughing.

"Don't choke on us." Melissa walked behind the bench and flicked me in the back of the head.

"Keep your hands off me." I took a swig of water. Melissa only wanted me alive so that she could kill me more publicly later on. If Morgan was here, she had even brought an assistant, or maybe just a witness. Either one would do. I decided to just bolt right after the game. They could say whatever they wanted about me, but I didn't have to be there to listen to it.

I needed to get home anyway. I couldn't stop worrying about Dad. I thought about the lit candles this morning and the smashed trash sculpture. What if he was walking along the highway looking for hubcaps and got too close to the edge? I remembered those speeding trucks and the way their air could push at you.

"Lindy!"

I jumped. Eric was behind the dugout, his hands through the chain link fence. "Hey," he said. "I just wanted to wish you good luck."

"Thanks." I put my fingers through the fence, just below his.

We had kissed twice more this week, once in an empty hallway and once outside behind the gym. But there was no privacy here. Gabby was stretching in the grass behind Eric. Jo was doing sprints. Kelly was relacing her shoes. And Melissa was swinging a bat in the cage just next to us, watching our every move.

Eric let his fingers drift down over mine. "There's something I wanted to ask you about." He looked down at the ground.

"It's a lie," I blurted. "Don't believe it."

"What?" He looked up at me.

Mrs. Tremont was calling us out on the field.

"What's a lie?"

"Gotta go."

"Lindy! What's a lie?"

I left Eric clinging to the fence and took my place at first base.

The game started badly. The leadoff batter singled and moved to second on a bunt. We could have handled that, but Melissa managed to drop an easy fly ball and then threw wildly toward third, and the runner scored. Dana looked like she was going to explode at Melissa. I walked over to the mound to calm her down. A strikeout and a fielder's choice finally ended Landsford's first inning, but they had jumped to an early lead.

I could hardly wait for my turn at bat. When it finally came, I strapped on my helmet and strode to the plate. I pawed the dirt like a bull getting ready to charge. Maggie

Vanderbright was on the mound for Lansford and she was the best pitcher in the league. She had three shutouts this year, but she wasn't going to get one today.

Gabby was on second with two outs. She had gotten a walk, and Kristin bunted her over to second. I was going to bring her home.

The first ball came in high, a sucker pitch that I am way too smart to go for. Ball one. I watched the next pitch fly toward the plate, lower this time, and I took a huge swing at it. The ball cracked hard against the bat, but my timing was off. It was a wicked line drive, but foul. It smashed against the chain link fence protecting the stands. I saw Morgan, in her bright orange Pickertown Pirates sweatshirt, flinch. Without the fence, maybe I could have gotten her. The fence wobbled with that musical clinking sound I love. One and one.

I stepped out of the batter's box and readjusted my grip. For a moment, I thought about hitting a pop-up over the fence. I imagined it falling smack into the nose on Morgan's upturned face. Blood would spurt everywhere. Morgan's nose would be so badly smashed that even the best doctors in the country couldn't fix it. She'd have to spend the rest of her life with an ugly, squashed nose. And when kids laughed at her, she'd think back to when she made fun of Ramón and Randy and me, and she'd be sorry.

"Ready, batter?" asked the umpire.

I swung a few extra practice swings, just to keep the pitcher waiting, and then stepped back into the box. The sun was hot, a hazy yellow ball hovering just above the trees to my left, and I could feel the sweat trickling down the back of my neck.

My teammates were cheering for me. "C'mon, Lindy!" "You got it, Lindy!" "Hit it out of here, Lindy!"

The next pitch was low and outside, and I let it go. I had to step out of the box again. It felt like a fog was growing inside my head. Two and one.

I took my stance. I could feel the grit of fine dirt between my teeth and the taste of it in the back of my throat. I was wondering how it got there when the ball whizzed by me.

"Strike two!" yelled the umpire. He was one of those loud ones, whose calls you can hear in the next state. His voice was going right through my brain. I thought about telling him to pipe down, but he might take it out on me my next at bat. Two and two.

The pitcher went into her windup and I focused on her, like a hungry tiger on its wounded prey. The pitch came in hard and fast, but right over the middle. It was mine. Rebecca flashed through my mind, and I took a home run swing. I heard the thump of the ball in the catcher's mitt and then a low groan from the crowd.

"Steeeerike three!" The umpire's call shot through my head like an arrow. I leaned on my bat for a moment and then dragged myself back to the bench.

"Nice whiff." Melissa shoved her shoulder into me as she headed out toward right field.

Kelly handed me my glove. "Don't worry about it, Lindy. You'll get it next time. Are you OK?" she asked. "You look . . . "

"I'm fine." I grabbed my glove and headed for first. But I wasn't fine. The fog was growing and my arms and legs felt heavy. I stood by the base in my defensive stance. Everybody else seemed like they were miles away and I was on my own planet.

It was the third inning when I saw him. Our team was at bat, and I was sitting on the bench watching my teammates strike out without so much as a foul tip.

"Look!" Melissa cried, so loudly that even the pitcher turned around on the mound. "It's that disgusting trash-picker guy!"

I felt something rip open inside me, and a hot, sharp pain settled into the bottom of my stomach. I sat very still and sunk my nails into the soft leather of my glove.

"He's waving at us!" Gabby shrieked.

"Eeewww!" Dana and Kristin sang in unison.

"Somebody should make him go away," Mae said, a fake tremble in her voice.

Mrs. Tremont caught my eye for just a second before I doubled over on the bench. I couldn't bear to look at her.

"Strike three!" the umpire called.

"Melissa!" Mrs. Tremont barked. "You're up! Why weren't you on deck, warming up?"

I bolted for the Porta Potti that was just behind the field in a small clump of trees. There were two outs and Melissa was up. I knew I didn't have much time. The smell gagged me before I could even open the door. I ran around the back, bent over, and threw up in the bushes.

"Strike two!" the umpire sang.

Evil thoughts filled my head — Melissa getting hit with a pitch, losing all her front teeth, losing everything she cared about. I leaned back against a tree, waiting for the weakness to go away.

"Lindy, are you OK?" Mrs. Tremont's head poked from around the side of the Porta Potti.

"I'm fine!" I spat and rushed past her. I am so tired of people asking me that question. Why can't people just leave other people alone?

"Lindy!" She grabbed me by the shirt.

"Let go!" I jerked free and headed for the field.

"I'm taking you out of the game." She said it in a quiet voice, but I heard her.

I whirled around. "No! You can't!"

"I can. You're worn out, Lindy. You're sick. You need to rest."

I wrung my hands together. "Oh, please, Mrs. Tremont, don't take me out," I begged. "I can play. I can make it. It's the last game."

She looked toward the field. Melissa must have made the third out. Our players were taking their positions. Dana was warming up on the mound. Mrs. Tremont let out one of those long sighs. "All right," she finally agreed. "We'll take it inning by inning. But I'll be watching.

Here, wipe your face. You've got a little something on your chin."

She handed me a handkerchief she had pulled from her pocket. I held it in my hand and stared at it.

"It's clean, Lindy," she insisted. "Go ahead."

But that's not why I hesitated. I was looking at the black letters stitched into the corner of the handkerchief — JWT.

I carefully wiped my face. "I'll wash it and give it back to you tomorrow."

"I'm not sure I really want it back now." She laughed. "Just throw it in the trash can and go grab your glove."

"But . . . it's . . . it's your husband's, isn't it?"

She put both of her hands on my shoulders and squeezed. "It's OK," she said. "I'm not sentimental about his handkerchiefs."

The umpire was looking at us impatiently. "Play ball!" he yelled.

Kelly flipped me my glove and I ran to first. Dad was leaning on the center field fence. He was wearing an old red flannel shirt and his blue jeans with holes in the knees. The afternoon sun seemed to make his long hair even more golden. I knew I should have run over to him. I should at least have called out to him to make sure he was feeling OK. All the outfielders were watching him. The crowd began cheering for Dana. I couldn't bring myself to even wave. I turned my back on him. I chewed on the inside of my cheek and concentrated on the batter.

19

◆ ◆ ◆

IN THE BOTTOM OF THE SIXTH inning, the score was still 1–0. It was my last chance to do anything. My last chance to be something. Maggie Vanderbright and the Knights were looking pretty smug with only two outs to go until they were the league champions. Then Gabby knocked a high pitch over the left fielder's head for a double. Maggie got rattled and walked Kristin on five pitches.

"We don't need a home run," Mrs. Tremont instructed, giving my arm a squeeze. "There's only one out. Just get your bat on the ball and bring Gabby home. Are you OK? Can you do this?"

"I'm fine, fine, fine," I mumbled. I stepped around the fence and into the batter's box. I could be a hero. Dad had spent much of the game pacing behind the outfield fence. Now, he stood still, in dead center, his hands in his pockets. Everyone, except me, had grown used to his presence. I don't think I heard even one rude comment about him last inning.

I swallowed hard and tapped my bat on the plate. I tried to steady myself, but it felt like the ground was moving. Maggie stared down at me from the mound. She waved off the first couple of signs from her catcher. Finally, she gave a quick, short nod and pulled back to throw. The ball slammed into the catcher's mitt.

"Strike one!" called the umpire.

I saw the catcher smile through her mask. But Maggie was still all concentration, as though she could strike me out with just her stare.

"Come on, Lindy!" called Gabby. "Bring me home! It's hot out here!"

It was hot. My whole body seemed to be melting. I wiped my face with the edge of my shirt. Perspiration was stinging my eyes.

Maggie agreed with her catcher on the first call. She wound up and fired. It was the exact same pitch as the first. It was in the catcher's mitt before I could even breathe.

"Strike twoooo!" called the umpire.

Maggie allowed herself a small smile. The catcher walked the ball out to the mound to talk over the next pitch. I stumbled out of the box. I knew people were calling things to me from all sides, but it all blurred together into nothing but a distant buzzing sound. It felt as if I were slowly disappearing from the earth. If I struck out here, I would disappear. I would have nothing.

As I stepped in toward the plate, I saw Dad. He was standing on something — I couldn't tell what — and he rose partially above the fence, his arms straight up in the air, all fingers pointing to heaven. He had the wrong sport, but I had to smile. We used to play "touchdown" in the old house with a little rubber football. You had to keep your hands up high as goalposts, but you could run anywhere. The player with the football had to chase you and fling the ball between the "posts" to get a score. It was fun, but sometimes we broke things. Even when I did it, he always took the blame.

I saw people in the stands looking at him. Maggie turned around briefly on the mound. He stood unmoving. He looked about ten feet tall. And for a moment, the fog left my brain. I gripped the bat. Maggie took her big windup and hurled the ball at me. I saw it clear as day, the whole way, almost in slow motion. I smacked it clean in the middle and watched as it sailed over the center fielder and just to the left of Dad's outstretched arms.

Gabby leaped into the air, over and over again, jumping rather than running toward home. Kristin almost caught her. My teammates were screaming, shaking and rattling the fence in front of our bench. I heard the crowd. But mostly, I heard Dad's whoop. He was pumping his fists in the air, cheering for me. I made it to second base, but third seemed so far away. I couldn't do it. I turned and headed toward center field. I fell just before I got to the fence. Next thing I knew, Dad had me in his arms. He picked me up, just like a baby, and held me. He carried me off the field and through the woods. I couldn't lift my head off his shoulder. I cried the whole way. I never made it around the bases, but I did make it home.

20

◆ ◆ ◆

I WAS SICK FOR ALMOST TWO WEEKS with some kind of flu. It was as if everything I had been keeping inside me for the past year had turned to poison and my body just couldn't take it anymore. I slept so much that I lost track of the days and nights. I have to admit that sometimes, in the very beginning of my sickness, I really didn't care if I ever woke up again. One day, in between the fevers and the sweats, when Mom and Dad were both in my room, I told them everything that I remembered about that day.

Dad was giving Rebecca a bath, and I was the only other one home. I was in my room, pretending to do my homework. But really I was reading a magazine. The phone rang and I ignored it. I was at a good part in a story about a girl who had anorexia. Dad called out to me. "Lindy, come stay with the baby while I get that phone." He was waiting for a call from work, about overtime.

"I'm coming," I answered, but not too loud, because the story was getting better. All I needed was about two minutes to get to the end of the article. So I kept reading. Dad and I got to the bathroom at about the same time. And we were both too late.

I didn't think it was real. It still doesn't feel real. Rebecca looked so peaceful, just like she was sleeping. I thought for sure that it was all a big mistake. I just knew that she was going to wake up. A person couldn't disappear from life just like that, could they?

Mom cried the whole time I talked, but she wasn't mad at me at all. She just kept smoothing her hand across my head and kissing me every sentence or two. She said it wasn't my fault at all and I was never to think that again.

Funny thing is, Dad didn't remember it the same way I did. He said he never called me to come watch Rebecca because he didn't even know that I was home. He insists I must have heard wrong, but I'm not so sure.

One thing I know for sure, though, is that neither one of my parents is the least bit mad at me. Every time I woke up those first couple of days, I saw one of them right next to my bed watching me and worrying. Dad told me lots of stories, too, like in the old days, and I was glad that they all had happy endings. Even though I know life's not exactly like that, it helps you keep your head up and hope for better things. And when I fell asleep, his stories filled my dreams and nursed me back to health.

Randy started doing his puzzles on the floor of my room. He is turning into quite a chatterbox. I hope I didn't hurt his feelings, but sometimes I fell sound asleep right in the middle of one of his long tales about who did what to who on the playground at recess. I think he's making some friends. Or maybe he had friends all along and I just never really listened before.

Even Freddy hung out with me sometimes and told me about the funny things some of the customers do at Eckles. Freddy's good at doing voices and he would act out whole scenes, making me laugh so hard that I was in danger of upchucking again.

And my friends? I guess I never gave them enough credit. Kelly, Gabby, and Dana came to visit me and they didn't act shocked or anything about where I lived. They didn't seem to care at all. Or maybe they just hid it real well. Dana brought a box of candy, and Kelly gave me a real cute teddy bear. I'll probably never be cool or popular, but I know that I have friends I can always count on.

Eric visited, too, and I just wanted to hide under the covers. I'm sure I looked beautiful, lying in bed, my hair all flattened to the sides of my head. But it was good to see him. He talked and laughed and told me stories about school just like he didn't even care about me living in this strange, dumpy house. And maybe he doesn't. There's a big seventh-grade dance at Mecong at the end of the year called the Spring Fling. And Eric wants me to go with him. I pretended I wasn't sure and I let him beg me a few times. He said he would bring me flowers and promised that we would have a really great time. I hope my mom will let me buy something new to wear.

I'm sure that by now everybody knows that I lived in a homeless shelter and that I lied about everything from my past. But I guess they didn't hold it against me too much. Mrs. Tremont stopped by one day to tell me that I had to get better because my teammates had voted me onto the all-star team. She told me at first that the vote was unanimous, but I didn't believe her. She finally admitted that it was really one vote short of that. That was OK. Melissa had signed the get-well card from the team, but if she had voted for me as an all-star, the shock to my system would have been too great and I would have gotten sick all over again. Kelly says that Melissa and Morgan are good friends now, and that's OK with me, too. They deserve each other.

My final hit did win the game for Mecong and we are the champions of our division. We get a banner to hang in the gym at school. I won't be getting my name on that plaque as the all-time home run champion, though. Seems that it doesn't count if you don't go around the bases and touch the plate. It's funny, but I don't care so much about that record anymore. Besides, there's always next year.

I asked Mrs. Tremont how her husband was doing. She said he was doing just the same, but she sure appreciated me asking about him. She talked about how much they had loved to travel, and she told me about all the cool places they had been. I was too afraid to ask what was wrong with him, especially when she was having so much fun talking about all their happy times.

I try to do the same with Rebecca. I still cry sometimes when I think of her, and Mom says that that's OK. But mostly, I try to think about the cute things she did and how she laughed all the time. I remember how she played hide-and-seek. She used to stand right in the middle of the room with her hands over her eyes. She thought that I couldn't see her, that just because she closed her eyes she was completely hidden. I still see Rebecca a lot, in my dreams and in my memory. I will always miss her.

Dad took down the mannequin-head pole. I told him that it freaked me out some days when I saw weird stuff on those shelves. He still works on his crazy sculptures, but that's OK. I think he just feels better when he has something to bang on. I hit softballs and Dad bends metal. I guess we all need something. It's kind of funny how I didn't realize that Dad wasn't the only one who went over the cliff after Rebecca died. At least we can work our way back up together. Dad says he's thinking of breaking with his tradition and going for a visit to the doctor — but only if I go with him. I think Mom must have put him up to it, but I guess it's not such a bad idea.

Mom promised that this summer I can go and spend a week with my friend Pauline in Philadelphia and visit with all my old crowd. I can't wait to tell Andy Carlucci about our softball championship and my "almost a home run" that won the game. I bet I had more home runs this year than he did. Those kids from Philly won't believe it when they hear about the giant houses and all the weird customs they have here in the suburbs. But I can tell them that the kids here are just the same as the ones from my old block — some are nice and some are real mean. I'm totally excited that I'm going back to Philadelphia for a visit. I know I'm not going to get to live there and that I can't have everything back just the way it used to be. But I think that I can have an OK life here in Shelbourne. The tractor-trailers still rumble past my window, but I'm so used to them now that I don't even hear them anymore.

In June I will turn thirteen years old. I grew up a whole lot in one year. Now I know most everything there is to know in this world. When you're eleven, you're just a baby. When you turn thirteen, you're practically a grown-up. In between, it's like a crazy upside-down roller-coaster ride. So hold on. It's scary and you want to scream a lot. But if you let it, it can be fun, too. And that's the truth about twelve.